GREEN TERROR

Chris Boult

New Generation Publishing

Acknowledgements

Thanks to all who continue to support me and have assisted in any way in bringing this fourth book to print. A special thanks to my son Jake for the initial read and critique and to Titanic Brewery for supporting the launch events.

Author's note

The story is set in the current era. All the characters are fictional, as are some of the places and all of the events.

We live in an increasingly uncertain world where the politics of inequality and scarcity, let alone ideology and religion all contribute to instability and insecurity.

Service in the army, a working life in criminal justice and following my son's experience of studying at Oxford, coupled with an interest in current affairs are the inspiration and basis for this story. New undergraduates meeting and becoming friends; destined for successful careers, how might they handle the conflicts, contradictions and dilemmas inherent in their future positions of power? Can they maintain their lofty ideals and aspirations to act in the public interest?

This is deliberately a relatively short read in an attempt to accommodate readers' busy lives.

'We never know the worth of water till the well is dry.'

– Thomas Fuller 1732

Chapter One

Cobra meeting, London

In a small, dark meeting room important matters were discussed; the very security of the nation, the balance of international diplomacy and the politics of pragmatism and compromise.

Towards the end of the meeting there was an interjection with new information.

'So, Nathan, what have we got?'

'This could be serious, Prime Minister,' replied his Private Secretary.

'Yes.'

'We have intelligence to suggest that the plane crash over South Africa last week wasn't due to chronic engine failure, but terrorist action. We believe this was a deliberate attempt to try to embarrass the British government over failure to make progress over certain international companies and unethical activity.'

'Yes, I see… and if your suspicion is right, would we be vulnerable?'

'Yes, Sir.'

'Um…' said the Prime Minister considering his position.

'I'm afraid we live in a very uncertain world, Prime Minister.'

'Indeed.'

Oxford

Oxford, one of the world's most prestigious universities, a national treasure and hallowed institution. Many of the country's leaders enjoyed their education in this eminent setting. What experience and contribution would this year's students make to the future of mankind and the development of civilisation?

Crichton marvelled at the sheer joy and splendour of the

Oxford skyline, even on such a dull morning. Heading out from college towards the river he waved a hello to Arabella as he left Radcliffe Square. With the lessons of ancient history going through his mind and the ever present concern about the future of the planet, Crichton crossed the road into Christchurch Meadow, following the path to the boathouses. Rowing was a major preoccupation at Oxford, although not for Crichton, for whom the privacy of the boathouse had more carnal implications. Walking along the path by the river, he spoke to the usual range of people sitting on the benches; the old, the lonely, the relaxed and the stressed out, as the wading birds rushed to the water to avoid his purposeful steps. Crichton had his head full of ideas he wanted to share and discuss with Ahmed and Conrad. Conrad was always on time and probably had already settled into his first lunch-time pint in The Crown, their favourite pub by the river. Ahmed, however, was more unreliable, and would probably be late as usual.

Crichton approached the garden of The Crown with a sense of boyish excitement. Crichton Broadhampton-Scott, attitudes and manners honed in the best of English public schools, was relishing the academic challenge and pure indulgence of studying History & Classics at Canterbury College Oxford. The college attended by both his father and grandfather and many members of his famous school.

Crichton was right that Conrad Lindstrand was already sitting comfortably in the garden overlooking the river. Educated in Sweden, Conrad always harboured an ambition to study abroad and was delighted to have been offered a place to study biology at Canterbury College. Environmental science was his major interest and he hoped to go on to research climate change and its implication for global politics.

'Crichton, sit down. Let me get you a beer!' said Conrad.

'No, no, you've nearly finished yours. I'll get them in… the usual, or shall I surprise you?'

As Crichton returned with two real ales in hand the two young idealists smiled and shook hands.

'Um, that's nice. What is it?' asked Conrad.

'It's one of the guest ales; from Titanic Brewery in Stoke-on-Trent apparently.'

'Where's that?'

'I don't know, is it in Yorkshire?' asked Crichton.

'The North anyway.'

'Certainly beyond the M25,' said Crichton. They nodded as they laughed.

'Um, tastes good, what is it called?' asked Conrad.

'Anchor.'

'Solid.'

'Yes, well grounded,' said Crichton, and they smiled and exchanged boyish glances. 'Conrad, have you been here long?'

'No, not really,' he said. 'I'm just thinking about presenting my paper this afternoon to the International Relations Society. It's about the case for radical action to avoid climatic catastrophe.'

'Really, how interesting. I feel so strongly about this too. Mainstream thinking and entrenched interests seem destined to ignore the growing weight of evidence that the world will soon be beyond the point of no return unless we act *now*. Conventional politics seems unable to deliver an answer; we need something more radical. What are we going to do?' said Crichton with conviction and great enthusiasm.

'Yes, I've been charting the likely impact of global temperature rises of one to five degrees centigrade and it's frightening.'

'Go on.'

'Well, the impact on food and water supplies, damage to eco systems, ever more erratic weather bringing flooding and major disruption could threaten our very cohesion and stability. Ultimately, this could lead to the breakdown of world order, leaving us to descend into chaos.'

'Chaos, did I hear chaos on such a lovely day as this?' remarked Ahmed, as he approached with a beer in hand. 'I assumed you two would have already started.'

3

'Indeed, the world won't wait for you Ahmed,' replied Crichton.

Educated in Saudi Arabia and the USA, Ahmed Salib was now studying Politics, Philosophy and Economics. Calmly, Ahmed sat down and joined the conversation as sharp young minds addressed serious intractable great world problems with diligence and determination.

The three young men had soon bonded on arrival at Oxford and found solace in a common interest about the future of the planet. They had researched well and debated many times, usually coming to the same conclusion that the time for conventional approaches had passed. A series of G8 conferences had produced lacklustre agreements over the years, which the signatories invariably failed to deliver. The next Paris conference was heralded to be no different.

Later at the International Relations Society, the small select group took their seats at the meeting eager to hear Conrad's thoughts about climate change. It was a popular topic amongst the Oxford scientific community and Conrad promised to be a significant thinker in the field. The Chair politely indicated that it was time to start and Conrad confidently presented a range of evidence.

'First, there is the debate about whether climate change is fantasy or reality: the deniers claim that there is no case to answer or the case has been massively overstated, versus those who believe the case is now unequivocal or established to some degree.

'Denial is undoubtedly convenient for certain vested interests, but its academic support and scientific basis is questionable. It appears to be based on attempting to deny the existence of evidence, dispute its contents or undermine its significance. I can find no plausible core data to support a case for consistency of key measurements over the centuries. There is an argument that vacillation in global climate is normal or beyond our control, and to assume that it is influenced by man – let alone caused by him – is presumptuous and arrogant. This line of argument takes us beyond science and into more fundamental philosophical or religious questions, beyond the scope of my presentation.

'To be more specific, I'd like to quote just a few pieces of evidence to support the case that climate change is real and dangerous, and to do so offer the following examples in relation to the changing pattern of water supplies:

'Data from NASA satellites on seventeenth January 2014, tracking world water reserves. Hydrologist James Famiglietti of the University of California concludes that California is on the verge of an epic drought with groundwater reserves critically low or on the point of running dry.

'Already across the world a billion people – one in seven of the population – lack access to safe drinking water.

'Rapid drying of all the world's major arid and semi-dry regions.

'Increases in the pumping of ground water to service agriculture over an area of two thousand kilometres, supporting a population of approximately six hundred million people over East Pakistan, Northern India and Bangladesh, are not sustainable. The convergence of falling supplies and growing demand compound the problem and shorten the timescale before it becomes critical and threatens to result in mass starvation.

'Similar concerns have been expressed in relation to the Nile, Tigris-Euphrates, Mekong, Jordan, Indus, Brahmaputra and Amu Darya water basins.

'The governments of Brazil, several Middle Eastern countries and China for example have all expressed concern about their capacity to plan and deliver water supplies to cities and agriculture in the coming years with Crown Prince General Sheikh Mohammed bin Zayed al-Nayhan of the United Arab Emirates saying: "For us, water is (now) more important than oil."

'Chris Rapley – a leading British scientist – predicts that a modest one degree rise in temperature would result in the disappearance of small mountain glaciers and a rise of three degrees would result in over a billion people suffering water shortage, mostly in Africa.'

Conrad continued to broaden his case, leading to questions and a lively discussion.

'Presumably the cause of these changes is rising global temperatures, Conrad?'

'Yes, I believe so. Each of the last three decades have been successively warmer than any previous decade since 1850, with the last thirty years from 1983–2012, being the warmest in almost fourteen hundred years.'

'Isn't it also true that decline of the arctic ice sheets, rising sea and ground temperatures could release catastrophic levels of CO_2 hitherto trapped beneath the sea, and in permafrost that could significantly accelerate the onset of disaster?'

'Yes,' was the sombre response leading to a reflective level of stunned silence, interrupted by the Chair reminding them that a special lecture was to be staged later in the week to outline the history of international initiatives to address this issue. He continued to say that it would go on to give a summary of the challenges facing the world leaders at the forthcoming Paris conference.

'Presumably that history of international effort is less than inspiring?'

'True, I'm afraid so,' replied the Chair confirming Conrad's conclusion before thanking him for his presentation. As members dispersed, the obvious question on their minds was: *What is to be done?* Individual or action at mere state level would be insufficient most concluded, but how to rise its profile, how to ignite international action, those were the real questions! Debate was lively as members trickled away to enlarge the numbers of students and academics in the various popular pubs and meeting places around Oxford.

The beer flowed and the debates continued well into the night.

Chapter Two

Friends of the Earth enjoyed a good history with Oxford University. The student Environmental Society made regular contact and exchanged information with various green lobby groups. Hilary Jameson was not mainstream however, even by the standards of Friends of The Earth. Green activists had a range of attitudes to how far direct action was justified and reasonable if in the pursuit of noble ends. Hilary was off the edge and prepared to do almost anything if she thought it was right. At times she clashed with those more conservative or as they would argue realistic leaders of Friends of the Earth, not that this had any impact on her beliefs and motivation, if anything it made her even more determined to be radical. In taking her cause to Oxford she saw the potential for meeting malleable young intellectuals and influencing future leaders, which she relished.

The Environmental Society had invited a speaker with extensive knowledge of disaster relief to address their forthcoming meeting. Crichton and Conrad were looking forward to hearing of his experiences. They walked across the city with a sense of expectation, passing familiar places, crossing busy roads, careful to avoid the ever present Oxford cyclists until they reached the meeting rooms. As they sat down they looked around them at the assembled group; academics, students, activists and a mixture of less readily identifiable people of mixed age, sex and race, they wondered what had drawn all these people's attention. As soon as Andre Debois from Save the Children started to speak, the audience were captivated and the motivation to attend the meeting was apparent. His real life accounts were of predictions ignored, agencies in denial, slow to react, under prepared and keen to take the credit by inflating the positives and burying news of the true scale of disasters; the loss of life, the impact on the local economy, housing, agriculture and infrastructure. There were gasps, tears and finally applause for the worthy representative. Some left inspired, but many left feeling angry.

Walking back to college the two friends were both quiet until a thought from either of them triggered a burst of condemnation or rage. What was this world they were about to inherit? What had previous generations done to it and why? Was the situation retrievable or was it all hopeless? The debate ensued with passion and intensity.

Also, walking home that night from the meeting were a man and a woman with very different interests. Crime was their trade, and they were looking solely to make money by any means. This experience offered food for thought on different avenues and means to expand their criminal empire and of people to watch who may climb the greasy pole and could potentially be useful later.

They observed, they noted and they reported back.

The following day the three friends were reviewing their impressions of the meeting with other students. Ruth Patel (Anglo-Indian), studying Mathematics, impressive, strong willed, and thought that any positive impact was admirable and that people shouldn't expect miracles... but others were far more critical.

'How can we make a difference?' posed Crichton.

'That is the central question,' replied Conrad, whose family were leading players in the world of Swedish environmental politics. He always intended to return to work in Sweden to devote himself solely to the cause, although unbeknown to him his fellow undergraduate Hayley Smith had rather different plans for him.

Following the theme of many a previous discussion, Conrad expressed his belief: 'We must commit to taking action, however small. Endless pontificating and debate is meaningless if ultimately we don't act.'

Conrad went on to outline some possible approaches with an impressive list of initiatives that he was aware of and how they could help in a tangible as well as a political sense to help take things forward.

'What are your plans post Oxford Ahmed?' asked

Hayley.

'I intend to return to Saudi Arabia, seek a position in government from where I hope to bring influence to bear.'

'Yes, but what does that actually mean?' she replied.

'You need to be patient, Hayley, politics is about the long game,' commented Ruth, entering the conversation.

'Yes, but do we have time and will it be enough to take things forward?' posed Crichton sombrely.

He often took on assumed responsibility for such issues. Coming from privilege, Crichton did feel a strong sense of responsibility to make a difference, and to change the world for the better. And whilst he felt proud to be in a position to do so, he also felt the burden of that expectation. The intensity of Oxford and its opportunity to think creatively with no boundaries was both stimulating and terrifying and Crichton admitted to struggling with his own demons at times. Not that such dilemmas and feelings were unusual amongst Oxford students.

Over the following term, Crichton and Conrad regularly attended fringe green meetings and built up their connections in the world of radical green politics. As they did so, their ambitions became more defined and their aspirations more extreme. Crichton's family had long planned a career in the Foreign Office for their favoured son. He was beginning to have his doubts, but as Ruth regularly reminded him, a man in his position would be well placed to further the environmental cause from within. Would that be enough for him? He wasn't sure.

It seemed that so much of his life had been predetermined: boarding school, constant supervision, moulding, guiding or suffocating? Maybe he should have had the confidence to break out. Meeting a wider range of people at Oxford – albeit mostly from a similar background – had opened his horizons to other possibilities. Perhaps to be a green crusader was his life's work, his destiny? He didn't know.

Ruth had experienced a similar privileged upbringing featuring nannies, nurseries and attendance at the best of schools. She had developed an inner confidence, a sense of certainty and a sense of her place in the world. She felt neither embarrassed by it or in any way uneasy. Prior to Oxford, Bath Ladies College had provided the finishing touches to a rounded transformation into a confident young lady ready to take on the world.

Crichton's phone signalled a text as he woke at 10.00am after a particularly good night's drinking in The Kings Arms – affectionately known as the KA – and The Turf. It was Conrad suggesting breakfast in their favourite café and then lunch at a discrete fringe green meeting. Crichton was due to meet Michael that lunchtime at the boathouse but knew that he could put him off and that he would understand. The others knew that Crichton was gay and were relaxed about it. His father on the other hand was a strong right wing Christian and prominent senior civil servant who would have no mention of even the possibility of homosexuality, least of all in his own family. Ruth was particularly understanding and very practical about such things. She had already identified Crichton as a possible contender. For her the choice of a potential husband was much more about position, influence and status than mere love or compatibility.

The two friends met somewhat hung over at the café and ordered the all-day breakfast with strong coffee. The fringe meeting was out of town and would involve a bus journey or a taxi ride. In their current state, neither felt inclined to cycle. Conrad suggested the bus as it was less conspicuous, which made Crichton laugh with thoughts of clandestine operations.

They stood at the bus stop in the rain and tried to summon up some enthusiasm for the forthcoming encounter. Whilst interested, Crichton had begun to think that maybe this obsession was getting a little out of hand and was adversely affecting his studies. Nevertheless, he bantered with Conrad about green politics and seemingly noble aspirations.

'If the government was serious about limiting carbon

emissions, they would have legislated years ago to force the car industry to instigate battery and hybrid cars much earlier.'

'Yes, the technology is all but there now, but still no impetuous to implement it.'

'Yes, but as ever pockets of progress would not be enough, this needs action on a global scale,' said Crichton.

'Quite.'

The bus arrived and they embarked, struggling with the inconvenient necessity of finding change to secure a ride to their destination in Cowley. The bus moved off as they laughed about how long it had been since either of them had used such artisan transport.

The meeting was a small affair, with various speakers, discussion groups and informal exchanges over tea. Actions were discussed, alliances forged and promises made. It seemed that the case for action was overwhelming and indecision was indefensible.

In the background Hilary Jameson observed and could sense the passion in the room.

'There are those two students I mentioned to you, Hilary,' said one of the conveners. *Yes,* she agreed, ones to watch, they could be useful in the future.

'Yes, they seem very bright and very committed,' said Hilary.

'How far do you think they would be prepared to go?'

'Oh I think a long way given the right encouragement.'

'Do we have anything on either of them yet?' she enquired.

'Yes, Hilary, actually I do. The one drinking his tea is Crichton Broadhampton-Scott. English gentleman, impeccable academic record, potential pillar of society and a felon.'

'Really, go on.'

'Yes he has a conviction for a public order offence, committed when he was eighteen. Apparently, he was already quite a radical before he came to our attention. At school he was active in protests in the local area, much to the annoyance of the school hierarchy, not to mention his father. It came to a head I understand when with others he confronted the local annual hunt. As you can imagine, the hunt saboteurs were keen to have acquired such a recruit. He fed them information about the hunt's plans, intentions, movements, that sort of thing, which they used to direct their protests. On one particular occasion, young Mr Broadhampton-Scott led a charge against the hunt at their rallying point, however, before they set off, the police were called and he ended up assaulting an officer.'

'Good man. Interesting, go on,' said Hilary.

'Uproar ensued between the family, the school and the surrounding hunt community. The land owner where the incident took place was the Chair of the school trustees and a local magistrate. Initially, apparently, he lobbied hard to have Crichton both expelled and charged with assaulting the officer, but was later persuaded to calm down in the interests of the school. Despite Crichton's protestations his father intervened at high level and the authorities – independently of course – agreed to accept a plea for leniency due to youthful over exuberance and went on to proceed with the lesser charge. Reassurances were extracted from Crichton, no doubt under duress from both the school and his father and the matter was effectively smoothed over and hushed up. Nevertheless, he has a conviction.'

'Um, surprising that,' replied Hilary sarcastically. 'Any more?'

'Yes, in the summer prior to going to Oxford, Mr Broadhampton-Scott attended a protest march in London where with others he attracted the attentions of the police Riot Squad.'

'So he'll be on their radar then?' asked Hilary.

'As a troublesome activist, yes I think so.'

'How about his friend?' asked Hilary with a sense of optimism.

'His name is Conrad Lindstrand. He's Swedish. He has no convictions as far as I'm aware, but certainly a history of involvement in radical politics.'

'So, he could be on the watched list, as it were, by the authorities both here and abroad?'

'Yes, Hilary, I think that's likely.'

'Well done. Thank you for that. These guys could be useful.'

Chapter Three

Romania

In a back room in a small town in Romania, a tight-knit group were meeting to discuss strategy.

'Any change in the overall picture, Jan?'

'No, Tak.'

'So, we are still successful in prostitution, people trafficking, fraud, gambling and money laundering; however, we need to expand operations if we are to hold our position and compete in this overcrowded market. Any ideas?'

One of the group spoke up.

'Yes, Tak, I've been looking into medical fraud.'

'Go on,' said Tak.

'Well, it's got massive scope; a world market desperate to grab at any chance of health and longevity at almost any price.'

'Sounds ideal. Have you taken it forward?'

'Yes, Tak, I have. We have been selling a certain anti-aging remedy. A recent report by the Human Longevity Panel – which is constituted to advise the insurance industry – has concluded that whilst there is disagreement about how far the maximum lifespan could increase, some experts foresee an achievable limit of about one hundred and twenty years, while others believe it could ultimately be limitless. Anti-aging pills are the new Viagra, they sell like hot cakes. There are some mad people in this market, really off the scale, green issue nuts, but I reckon we can keep below the radar and not be detected for a while.'

'And do they work?' asked Tak.

'Of course not, at least not ours.'

'But do they cause any harm?'

'No, no more than an extra sugar in your tea, Tak.'

The group laughed as Tak was known for his sweet tooth.

'There you are,' said Tak addressing the group. 'Initiative! So, what are your sales figures, Jan?'

'Cost per tablet ten pence. Sale price one pound, which equates to ninety per cent profit with sales approaching a million in three months, Tak.'

The room fell silent.

'A relative gold mine.'

'Precisely.'

Oxford

Michael had forgiven Crichton for changing their date. They met to walk together by the river. Michael was concerned that Crichton was spending too much time chasing his green aspirations, which added to Crichton's own misgivings. The couple were close but both knew that in the long term it was hopeless. Prejudice, family pressure and career ambition were destined to keep them apart, but for now they could enjoy their time together in relative security. Crichton had always felt that he was different. It was not just the excessive amount of time spent in male company in the close intensity of a private boarding education, but a feeling of comfort beyond mere availability that had suggested to him that he was gay. Crichton was not regarded as a 'pretty boy' at school and had not attracted the attentions of staff, but he did remember enjoying a brief encounter with a sixth former when in the third form, which at the time he regarded as a normal part of the fagging system. It was not until life in Oxford that Crichton was actually exposed to female company to any significant degree and he found it most strange. Interesting, however, that he did feel comfortable with Ruth, but not attracted to her.

Ahmed was missing home. Although quite well travelled and partly educated in the USA, he struggled with the Englishness of Oxford and of course the weather. At home he would have real status and would automatically take his place in the senior ranks of state control without difficulty.

It was his birthright and education was not required as a route to power, although he felt that it would help, certainly with dealing with those from the non-Arab world. He envisaged a life of comfort and privilege, and he looked forward to it. In the immediate term, however, there was Oxford, and pride alone motivated him to aim high for he knew he could not buy a degree, so he had to work for it. His association with Conrad and Crichton was pleasant enough, but transient he thought. As regards commitment to the 'green battle', at times he admitted to himself that Conrad and Crichton's relative enthusiasm and sheer naivety irritated him. Nonetheless, he did feel some responsibility to change the world for the better, but only in part; after all, the green agenda didn't sit easily with his vast family holdings in Middle Eastern oil.

Later, Ahmed saw Crichton in the library and suggested lunch. This time they did take advantage of the college facilities, which were good quality and heavily subsidised if a little inflexible. They talked again about world affairs, great philosophical ideas and their political applications.

'Do you envisage war over food and water shortages, Ahmed?' asked Crichton.

'In time I think it's inevitable, yes.'

'And the poor will fair the worst.'

'Yes, also inevitable. The powerful will pontificate but fail to act while the poor suffer,' said Ahmed.

'Over population also presents a challenge doesn't it, Ahmed. Yesterday, I was reading an article about human aging. Nir Barzilai, director of the Institute for Ageing Research, is sceptical about some of the upper estimates but still accepts that human kind could well live to around one hundred and twenty in the foreseeable future. Imagine the social and geo political implications of that!'

'Yes, it certainly would add to any existing pressure on resources, including food and water if we all start living another twenty to fifty years.'

'Where will we all live, Ahmed? The earth's a small planet. Do you ever think that there must be other inhabitable planets out there with scope for human colonisation?'

'Yes, I do, but don't expect a panacea. And realistically, even if available, would it not be just an escape route for the rich and powerful leaving the rest to struggle on a planet bereft of resources?'

Just as they were getting up to leave, Arabella joined them. Arabella Taylor-Shaw was stunningly beautiful, marvellously rich and tremendously talented, who had been educated in London in various international private schools. She was, however, from new money and had a shrewder take on privilege, earned or otherwise. Arabella envisaged her role as more of a celebrity than a business women and she wasted no time in promoting her ambitions, meeting the right people, sleeping with some of them and avoiding others. She was ambitious, energetic and capable.

'Are you boys saving the world again?' she enquired. 'How very tiresome of you.'

'Arabella, we were just leaving to return to the library, shall we see you later?'

'You may, Ahmed, darling, you may,' she replied with a glance that could melt any man's heart.

'Are you going out?' Crichton asked as they walked away.

'No, not yet anyway, but isn't she lovely,' said Ahmed.

'Yes she is, for a woman,' said Crichton, and they laughed.

***

Over the middle term Ahmed and Arabella did spend more time together and made a charming couple. Quite a match, thought Ruth, although personally she felt much happier with the prospect of Crichton. And while she still hadn't taken the trouble to inform him, Ruth was used to getting what she wanted and perceived of no possible resistance.

Hayley Smith on the other hand was a rare Oxford animal, one who could genuinely claim to have come from 'an ordinary background'. Although Oxbridge claimed to have made progress in recruiting the most able from all backgrounds, the reality was somewhat different. Most undergraduates came from a handful of private schools and were largely southern, if not London based. The figures suggested otherwise as they included under state schools a small elite group of state sponsored grammar schools, which were more akin to public than 'ordinary' traditional state comprehensive schools. Of course, the landscape was also changing due to the growth in free schools, which somewhat clouded the picture. Hayley had gone to a very standard state comprehensive in a rough part of Leeds and was probably the only girl ever to have secured a place at Oxford from her school. She knew that she would never have made it had a young teacher – ex-Cambridge himself – not recognised her rare potential early. It was he who had encouraged her, helped her believe it was possible and coached her through the application process, a standard service of course in most public schools.

Hayley was realistic, hard headed and did not harbour any feelings of inferiority. She was proud of her humble beginning but did not see herself as some working-class heroine on a mission. She recognised that she had earned an opportunity against the odds and fully intended to make the most of it. She avoided much of the Oxford elitist social culture but thoroughly enjoyed the level of academic stimulation and challenge. Her tutors soon recognised her potential and she was earmarked for a first early on in her academic career.

Hayley was fascinated by some of the people around her. At home she had found most of the local boys to be 'chavs and dickheads' and was not impressed with their fascination for Leeds United, warm larger and soft drugs. She had particular feelings for Conrad and was not shy in making it known to him. Initially, he had resisted but she had persevered and their relationship was now well established. He did wonder where this would leave his future plans of a return to Sweden. Hayley could see him as a potential route out of the depressing blandness of the background that she had come from. A talented linguist she taught herself Swedish in her spare time and hung on to the hope that maybe Conrad would invite her to return home with him at some point.

Chapter Four

New York

Brad Maier was sitting in his office with a coffee, the usual strong espresso, staring through the window of his high-rise office into the clear blue sky.

Brad, an ex-Oxford graduate himself, had been recruited by the intelligence community whilst at college. He specialised in Middle Eastern affairs and spoke several languages fluently, including Arabic.

He was working on a given project when connections started to appear in his mind and a certain level of alarm ensued. Monitoring long-term trends was actually quite boring he thought, but every so often something more tangible occurred to raise the pulse. What was he seeing and what did it mean he wondered?

Yemen

The world of Islamic terrorism was complex. Many groups and sub groups existed, but at worst in some quarters it was believed that such groups were committed to the widespread installation of extreme regimes and ultimately the overthrow of the West, or at least to challenge the dominance of the West over world affairs.

ISIS had successfully exploited the West's weakness and indecision in shying away from open confrontation. The aftermath of 9/11 and the Iraq war that followed had left a bitter taste of misjudgement in the minds of the key leadership of most Western states, particularly and crucially America where president Obama had made his position abundantly clear that he had no intention of committing American boots on the ground in any attempt to take on ISIS, or any other emerging radical Islamic fundamentalist organisation, at least not openly. Tactics emerged to fit the new political mindset that conventional war was off the agenda and more indirect and less risky alternatives were in favour.

Meeting in Yemen, the leadership of a loosely aligned group explored the reasons for their success and how they might continue their campaign. Imposing elements of what the West referred to as Sharia Law had been successful in parts of the Middle East and North Africa, leading to the relative dominance of ISIS. Their attention was now turning to extending influence and attacking the West more directly. Ideas were traded, assessed, discarded or referred on to experts for further consideration and development. For them, however, one positive aspect emerged loud and clear. There existed a whole network of sympathetically minded people across much of Europe and beyond, sleepers effectively, ready for action if called upon to fight Jihad.

New York

'Chas, I have to talk to you urgently,' demanded Brad of his immediate superior.

'OK, my office five minutes.'

Brad gathered his papers and wondered if he was over reacting or whether he was being too cautious? He wasn't sure, but one thing he was sure about was that he had to share the information that had just come to his attention.

He stood outside Chas's office and tried to keep calm while he waited to be invited in.

'Brad, come in and sit down. Coffee?'

'Chas, let's talk first.'

'OK talk.'

'Chas, it occurs to me that we have had a number of indications now from a variety of sources to begin to suggest that ISIS have moved beyond general statements and posturing, to actually planning a direct attack on the West. Now, at this point this appears to be mere intention and does not include chapter and verse of what, when and how, but I do believe that we need to take this seriously and start making preparations to counter the threat.'

'OK so far, but you appreciate it's all pretty vague, Brad, so what's new?'

'Well, over the last six months there has been a noticeable increase in the numbers of migrants successfully crossing the sea from North Africa to Europe. Many of those people are never caught, processed or tracked in any way. Given the consistency of reports from police and state intelligence organisations, I believe a pattern emerges of growing numbers of potential operatives deliberately planted in the West. For what I ask myself?'

'Well?' invited Chas.

'The scope is wide isn't it? We couldn't possibly track all these people, some perhaps many may well disappear off the radar. There are also reports of suspicion of building weapon stockpiles as well as what we know about terrorist training camps. Chas, if we don't address it we risk losing the battle before it's started!'

'Um, a little dramatic, Brad. When did you last take some leave? Perhaps a short break would do you good?'

Cornwall

Hilary Jameson was planning a campaign, timed to have maximum impact on the eve of an important speech by the Prime Minister about a revision of policy on climate change. The concern in the green community was that the speech would sound tough and attempt to convey action on a number of fronts that in reality meant very little if not the watering down of already compromised limp commitments.

Appearing to be proactive was deemed to be politically prudent in advance of the Paris summit. British relations with European leaders, at least within the EU, remained difficult at times and the Prime Minister was desperate to be seen to be taking a lead. The press office was buzzing the speech writers had excelled themselves.

The media were ready, primed and briefed to report a good news story. The Prime Minister was expected to announce plans to build a new reservoir in Cornwall to meet anticipated future needs, funds for further research on harvesting drinking water from the sea by desalination, and a longer-term plan to link water supplies by use of pipes, rivers and canals to form an integrated national network. This was to be presented as a brave and innovative approach to investing in future 'resource security' and to be ahead of the intentions of all other political parties. What he wasn't going to mention was the planned delays in funding until after the next general election and some abuse of statistics to present some existing funding commitments from European money to appear to be new.

Music to Hilary's ears, a few small drops could make a massive difference she was assured, and just at the right time to steal the headlines.

**

A major incident plan was soon sanctioned with coordination between police, health and military authorities in response to the apparent poisoning of the water supply in West Cornwall. Reports had been coming in for the last few hours of cases of severe vomiting and paralysis with links made to drinking water. Water samples were being taken quickly across Cornwall to try to establish any common cause.

The Prime Minister's speech went ahead as planned, but the media response was all about the attempt to poison the water supply and the political capital expected from his announcement was lost. The Prime Minister was reported to be furious and looking for someone to blame. *Why when I have all these officials and state agencies can a bunch of flaming amateurs breach our civil security and cause chaos and apparently no one knows anything about it let alone is able to anticipate or stop it,* he thought.

Cobra, London

The mood was sombre as the Prime Minister received

23

reports of the recent events in Cornwall.

'Prime Minister, I can confirm that the local water supply in Cornwall was compromised by a formula that induced immediate vomiting and temporary paralysis. Intelligence suggests that this was the deliberate action of extreme green activists whose intention was to manipulate the media in order to distract you from your announcement yesterday,' said the Prime Minister's chief political advisor.

'Yes, and they succeeded, didn't they? How could this happen? Who are these people?' demanded the Prime Minister.

'A mixture of radical extremists, Sir.'

'Yes, obviously, but how far does their influence and support stretch?'

'Well, Sir, there is some evidence to suggest connections with student activists at Oxford.'

'My goodness, and academics?'

'No, Sir, not at this stage.'

'OK, at least that's reassuring, but do follow up the link with students. We don't want our valuable young people being drawn into such extremism. And your assessment?'

'Yes, Sir, as the green group has pointed out, their actions illustrate a strategic weakness, which would be easy to exploit and unfortunately made more so by any effective attempt to build an integrated national water network. In short, with the right dosage, an enemy could conceivably poison the whole population.'

'Yes, well that can't be allowed to happen and, gentlemen, all of you must ensure that it doesn't,' the Prime Minister insisted whilst banging the table before an abrupt conclusion to a tense meeting.

Meanwhile in New York, Yemen and Romania, interest was aroused.

Chapter Five

'This is the six o'clock news from the BBC, our main story tonight: police forces across Cornwall and the South of England have completed a series of dawn raids targeting green activists believed to be implicated in yesterday's poisoning of the water supply in Cornwall. The Prime Minister has made a statement in the House of Commons and was immediately supported by all other major party leaders. He stated that this incident may have been perceived to be a political act, but it threatened the very security of our nation and those responsible could be assured that the full force of the law would be brought to bear to track them down and bring them to justice...'

'Oh shit, they could be on to us!' cried out Crichton. *It wasn't meant to be this serious.* Immediately, he picked up his phone to call Conrad, and for a moment he wondered whether or not his phone had been tapped. However, after ridiculing the idea, he called him.

'Conrad, I'm worried. Have you seen the news?'

'Yes, don't panic, Crichton,' came the less than reassuring response.

'But this could involve us!'

'Come on, Crichton... we are only on the edge, stay calm.'

'What if they get at Michael; he couldn't take interrogation!'

'Crichton, we are not in some tin-pot third world country where people are interrogated, tortured, taken and disappear! Why would they involve Michael anyway, he's not been involved in this whole green affair with us?'

'To get to me of course!'

'Crichton, I really think you are going overboard on this. We are a long way down the chain, and after all, we are in a democratic country and have done nothing wrong. We are making legitimate over chores, that's all.'

'No, no of course, alright, alright... but they might not

see it that way.'

Crichton felt a little better but he was still on edge.

The following day the Oxford machine became aware of the implication of student interest in green affairs potentially going too far, and acted as you would expect with calm and confident ease to reassure the watching world that the dreaming spires were not a hot bed of terrorism. The Principal instructed all tutors to selectively have a quiet word with any student considered to be at risk of anything akin to 'radicalisation'.

The BBC news announced the arrest of Hilary Jameson. In Oxford, attempts were soon made to place distance between the unfortunate actions of a few over zealous extremists and any consequent bad publicity that might reflect badly on the university. In the immediate aftermath, all matters green went very quiet, posters were spirited away, meetings cancelled and calm restored.

The next day a police presence was evident around the university and discrete enquiries were made with 'the full cooperation' of the university authorities. The Principal called his inner circle and banged on about loyalty and college history… much that they had all heard before about being loyal to the Crown and the state since being formed in 1645. It was essential to remain calm; the integrity of the college was of prime importance, however, it was necessary to get these troublesome police officers off the site and back to chasing crime as soon as possible.

All went very quiet at first until Crichton burst into Conrad's room and announced: 'Conrad, Ahmed has been arrested!'

'Oh no, they haven't just made the obvious assumption have they?' he posed rhetorically.

'What do you mean?'

'Come on, Crichton… sometimes for an intellectual you are so naïve. Ahmed happens to be an Arab, so in the simplistic eyes of the authorities he has to be a terrorist, or at least a suspect.'

'What! But he's not. None of us are! I'm worried,

Conrad. What will happen now? What will my father think?'

'You'll have more to worry about than what your father thinks if this goes, how do you say, tits up. Now calm yourself, and if the police want to talk to us, then that's fine. We have a keen and legitimate interest in green politics, but know of no criminality or criminal intent, and certainly have no connection with this Hilary Jameson.'

'Yes, but can we trust the police on this? Don't they have all sorts of powers that they could use against us?'

'Crichton, I really don't think we are that big a consideration to them.'

'So why arrest Ahmed? Won't they see his involvement in politics as radical agitation, a public order or national security issue, not a matter of conscience or justice?'

'Yes, they might well,' said Conrad, 'but we can't influence any of that. I suggest we just stay cool and wait to see what happens. There's no point in getting in a flap at this stage. If the police want to interview us, then so be it; we've done nothing wrong and have nothing to hide.'

'Yes, OK. I hope you are right, Conrad. Thank you. A pint?'

'I think so. The Turf?'

'Yes. Morse might inspire us.'

***

Ahmed was coolness itself as the police tried to enquire, to suggest, to twist and turn in the hope of tripping him up, but he gave nothing away and gave no grounds for continued suspicion. After a short interview and suitable reassurances about passports and contact details, he left the police station to return to his room. Whilst outwardly calm he was inwardly seething; how could they make such simple assumptions? How dare they question him in such a manner! Ahmed was angry, very angry and anger didn't help. He didn't attempt to call the others, and for that significant moment, he felt very much alone.

27

Crichton and Conrad enjoyed a convivial pint and regained some sense of proportion, before returning to college for a good night's sleep in the hope that some semblance of normality would emerge by the morning. Meanwhile, the authorities were busily compiling a list of those believed to be involved or connected to radical politics.

The following day both Crichton and Conrad were woken earlier than usual by the college authorities and invited to dress quickly in order to assist the police with their enquiries. They were taken by car to separate police stations to be questioned. This was a new experience for Crichton, who had been flanked by two burly police officers in the back of a smelly old police car, without the slightest notion of who had been sat there before. A mass murderer perhaps, a sex offender, a shoplifter…? He was then taken to a place of their choice without any explanation, which to him was most unusual. *The sheer indignity!* And he wondered how this might affect his career.

After customary introductions and appropriate use of the desk tape recorder, the Chief Inspector spoke clearly but firmly to Crichton.

'Now, Mr Broadhampton-Scott, you have nothing to worry about. I want you to relax and simply help us with our enquiries. Can you tell me what interest you have in green politics, the places you attend and the people you meet?'

The *nice guy technique* Crichton thought. He explained in a flat-footed way how he envisaged a greener, fairer and more just world and how involvement in green politics was the only logical, mature and responsible way to proceed.

The Inspector seemed to listen at first and then glaze over as it became obvious that Crichton was not answering his question.

'More specifically, Mr Broadhampton-Scott, or can I call you Crichton, where do you meet in Oxford and who else is involved?'

Crichton spluttered: 'Well, we meet in a variety of

places, all legitimate meeting venues. What are you implying, Inspector?'

The Inspector ignored his provocation. 'Who do you meet with?'

'There are far too many to name them all, Inspector, and different people are involved in different groups.'

'Yes, I understand that, your two close University friends, Conrad and Ahmed, attend with you.'

'Well yes,' said Crichton, but as friends we have common interests. That's not a crime is it?'

After further probing questions the Inspector seemed resigned to his superficial cooperation and released him – at least for the time being.

For Conrad, however, it was somewhat more intrusive. He was a foreign national, although Sweden was hardly known for radical politics. But maybe that was the point posed by the interviewing officer? Conrad didn't bite; instead, he gave an eloquent explanation of his motivation and, after given suitable assurances, he was finally released.

Over the following days other members of the Oxford community were questioned in an attempt to build up a picture of who were involved and who, if anybody, were the key players. It also became apparent that two people had now died as a result of the poisoning, adding a further degree of seriousness to the investigation. The police posted boxes around the college giving opportunities for passage of confidential information, much to the irritation of the Principal, who thought it was tasteless and impertinent.

Ruth responded with confidence in her interview leaving the officer in no doubt about how she saw things in connection with her relationship with her three friends.

'Chief Inspector, I'm sure as a man of the world you are far more balanced than certainly Crichton and Conrad, who are just high-spirited boys, full of ambition and naïve good intentions. However, they are not a threat to anyone, I can assure you.'

'And you?'

'Naïve or a threat? No not I. I am a realist, Chief

Inspector. The world is fundamentally unfair, unjust and at times brutal and cruel, but that is beyond my influence. I intend to make my way in the world with as little effort as possible and have no interest in side shows like green issues or indeed politics whatsoever.'

'And Ahmed?'

'I know him less well.'

'Go on,' said the Chief Inspector.

'Well, he is an Arab after all, Chief Inspector. I choose my friends carefully and I don't need the likes of him.'

The interview concluded and the officers shared their impressions.

'Pure bitch. I wouldn't want to get in her way, Chief.'

'No, Sergeant, I agree,' said the Chief Inspector. 'But she's lying. Is she trying to protect Ahmed or herself, I wonder? Either way, I don't see her as a threat, although she seemed happy to distance herself from Ahmed. I think we need to get him in again.'

'OK, Sir, I'll see to it.'

Later that day Ahmed was arrested again and held under terrorist legislation for three days, whilst being questioned in various high security police stations in London. Intelligence officers fully investigated his family and background, looking for any suggestion of past links to fringe political groups or to terrorism. But to no avail. The process was thorough in the interests of national security and public protection, but did nothing to endear Ahmed to the British state or to the establishment.

The Crown

The following day Conrad, Crichton and Ahmed met for lunch in The Crown, all relieved to be away from police attention. Ahmed was quiet, Conrad reflective and Crichton hyperactive. They exchanged experiences of their police interviews and laughed and felt confident that nothing would come of it. But Ahmed was still angry. Crichton described a rare conversation with his father, who was livid at the implied slur to the family name.

'Does that concern you, Crichton? I mean, your relationship with your father?' asked Conrad.

'Frankly, Conrad, I don't give a fuck, I hardly know the man. I haven't lived with him since I was three when I was first sent away to school. He's my financier though, always has been and for that I still need him.'

'And that's it?'

'Pretty much, what else is there?' asked Crichton.

'Will your family know about this, Ahmed, or be concerned?' asked Conrad.

'No, my family would not belittle themselves by involvement in such petty matters.' Although unbeknown to him, some quite high level diplomatic exchanges had taken place with family representatives complaining bitterly about his treatment.

They changed the subject, had another pint and even started to think about the first year exams.

***

Under questioning, Hilary Jameson stoically refused to name or incriminate anyone else, much to the frustration of the officers involved. However, at local level the Oxford police had a positive statement from one of the local activists that both Crichton and Conrad were present at a local meeting attended by Hilary. *Was this significant?* they wondered. *Was this a link?* It seemed possible but it was tenuous. It was in fact the only scrap of evidence against them that could possibly link them with the incident in Cornwall, but it in itself was thought insufficient to bring a prosecution, yet it was logged both on police and MI5 files. It was intelligence.

Hilary Jameson was charged with serious terrorist offences and was destined for the full vengeance of the state represented by a very long prison sentence, and the state inevitably got its way.

31

Chapter Six

Soon the media and police interest in Oxford and terrorism moved on to other more topical stories, and a return to 'normality' resumed under the watchful eyes of the Principal. The university authorities did, however, interview the three students themselves to seek their commitment to peaceful politics, the integrity of the college and the security of the state. All three felt most uncomfortable with this approach, more so than during the police interviews, and that it was both unnecessary and disproportionately intrusive. Still, all were warned very firmly indeed that no protest or further comment was to be made at any time either now or in the future, if they still aspired to graduate. Crichton readily acquiesced largely out of fear of his father's reaction and of being cut off financially; Conrad found it all very English and actually too trivial to warrant serious concern, but Ahmed was incensed by it and narrowly avoided a confrontation with the Dean, however, thought better of it. Nevertheless, the whole affair left him with a very bitter sense of resentment against the English authorities. Shortly after that the term drew to a close and the summer break soon followed and a chance to move out of the Oxford bubble.

The familiar ritual was conducted with the usual aplomb, as anxious parents gathered to escort their treasured offspring back to the sanctity of home. Rooms were emptied ready for the conference season. Processions of families moved with ant-like efficiency to carry the paraphernalia of study to waiting cars. Goodbyes were said as the fleet of Volvos, BMWs and Range Rovers proceeded along the dual carriageway out of Oxford to meet the M40 at junction 9. The convoy then turned south to return to London and the Home Counties, with just the odd exception of the occasional Fiesta and Astra turning north to England's industrial heartland.

***

After suitable recuperation the students returned in October for their second year. Ahmed had made brief mention of recent events back home but was soon encouraged to see the bigger picture and not to derail his future over such a minor affair. Conrad had returned to Sweden for much of the summer and proudly taken Hayley with him. He was amazed by her confidence and her spoken word. She had managed to keep her Swedish studies a secret from him so he was amazed as he introduced her to his family that she launched into fluid Swedish much to their enchantment. She merely reminded him afterwards that as a fluent speaker of eight languages simply learning another one was not a problem. After her Swedish adventure financial necessity forced a return to Leeds for the remainder of the summer to work in the local café, where she first started working when she was fifteen years old. After a few weeks her father took her to one side and said to her in all seriousness that after she had finished at Oxford and come back home, if she played her cards right, he could see her running that café in a few years' time. She hadn't the heart to shatter his delusions. She didn't see many openings for an international translator in a café in Leeds after all.

Crichton idled his summer away between the family flat in London and the retreat in the Highlands, with only passing interest in joining the family yacht as it tiresomely sailed around the Greek islands again. Matters green were never mentioned of course, although Crichton discovered on his return that his father had made him introductions to a variety of more 'suitable' university societies to occupy his spare time more constructively. He was amused and did actually engage in Scottish country dancing and clay pigeon shooting, but drew the line at the Bullingdon Club.

Text and email messages over the summer ensured some coordination of arrangements for the following year, including securing accommodation in Jericho and an early reunion in The Crown for a welcome beer.

'Conrad, my dear chap, you look so pale! The Swedish forest no doubt,' said Crichton warmly.

'Yes, by contrast you look almost as tanned as Ahmed after no doubt a tour of the sun spots of Europe.' replied his friend.

'You'd be surprised actually.'

'If you two have quite finished I'll get the beers in and a bottle of fizz. Ruth, Hayley and Arabella promised to join us later,' stated Ahmed authoritatively.

'Excellent,' replied Crichton.

'Oh, how are things with Michael?' Conrad enquired discretely.

'Over, I'm afraid,' said Crichton instantly closing the subject.'

Pint followed pint including a variety of guest ales; one from a Welsh micro brewery and another brew from Titanic in Staffordshire. Stories were exchanged before eventually the girls arrived, Arabella and Ruth soon followed by Hayley. More drinks followed before a short taxi ride to Jericho to sample the pad that Ahmed had bought and was sharing with Crichton and Conrad. Rooms were spacious and ample to share and renew affection and expend sexual energy for those who were inclined and willing.

Their second year started at pace with early reminders of their need to commit to private study and start to both plan for their exams and their future careers. Many opportunities and contacts were available to them all through the extensive network of previous graduates offering guidance in a wide variety of professions.

Ruth and Crichton developed their mutual understanding and recognition of the suitability of a future match. Both families seemed delighted and Ruth was very open about her plans and expectations at least to him. She wanted a marriage of convenience to allow her scope for her own life and loves with the security of convention and mutual influence and wealth. Having said that she was also warm and affectionate and had a genuine regard for Crichton and an acceptance, more than tolerance of his nature. For his part Crichton loved her dearly in his own way and was more than happy to accept her proposal on her terms.

For Ahmed and Arabella, however, their match was more complicated. There were powerful cultural influences at play. Ahmed knew that his family would expect him to return and that a suitable bride would be found for him. He knew that the thought of trying to introduce a Western woman into his family would be virtually impossible, but he didn't want to lose her. Arabella enjoyed their relationship but suspected that any long-term commitment would be difficult and complicated, but for now why worry, life was too exciting! Arabella was more than capable of making her way in the world of fashion, design and media and she intended to enjoy the ride.

Academic life continued with the endless round of lectures, reading, tutorials and essay production interspersed with trips to The Crown, walks along the river and for Crichton of course, Scottish country dancing. In all their interests matters green had taken a back step with at times less than subtle influence being brought to bear by the university authorities to restrict any re-emergence of political activity. Most of the leading local activists had moved on after the investigation and Hilary Jameson was destined to be incarcerated for a very long time. Sitting in the beer garden at The Crown, the friends reflected on recent events.

'Lovely day to be free isn't?' posed Crichton, looking out at the open view across the river.

'Yes, we are lucky to be in this privileged position,' replied Conrad.

'It didn't turn out so well for everyone. I wonder what happened to the various people you used to meet through green activism?' asked Hayley.

'I don't know,' replied Crichton uncomfortably. 'They all seem to have moved away, hopefully to continue the fight elsewhere.'

'Didn't some of them get sent to prison?' asked Hayley.

'Yes, I think they did, the vengeance of the state

prevailed,' responded Crichton.

'Maybe, but you can't just go around poisoning people and expect there to be no consequences,' interjected Arabella.

'It was Hilary Jameson who was really hammered, wasn't it?' said Hayley. 'Didn't she get twenty years or something like that? Did you know her, boys?'

'No, we never met, but we knew of her,' said Conrad. 'Campaigners who challenge the system are more heroes than villains as far as I'm concerned.'

'Yes, if no one raises difficult issues or challenges the status quo then nothing moves forward,' said Crichton. 'Mahatma Ghandi, Emily Pankhurst, William Wilberforce, to name but a few… none of these people would have been popular with the authorities at the time.'

'Jesus Christ indeed,' added Ruth.

'Yes, there has to be times when in order to make progress you have to be unconventional, a little radical, and that pushing of the boundaries will inevitably incite unpopularity in certain quarters.'

'Yes, but, Conrad, that doesn't justify poisoning people! It could have been mass murder of the innocent, people who had no connection with green politics who just happened to turn their tap on. That sort of random slaughter can't be justified and, had it worked, wouldn't have advanced your precious green cause one jot! Indeed, all the publicity and power of the state would have been directed into tracking everybody and anybody down to be held to account. All of you could have attracted lengthy prison sentences… so grow up and get real!' proclaimed Arabella bringing the discussion back down to earth, as Ruth nodded her approval.

The friends maintained their interest in green affairs, however, and continued reading and researching information, still hoping to make a difference at some point in their lives. For now, this was a fading priority. The aftermath of the event in Cornwall had dampened their enthusiasm, despite continued debate between their response as mature pragmatism verses feeling that they had sold out at the first hurdle and should be ashamed of themselves. At such times Ruth and Arabella would usually be able to lighten the subject and ease their consciences. Ruth the pragmatist could always state a case for compromise and make it sound statesman like, and Arabella would just say something real that distracted the conversation and made them all laugh.

Chapter Seven

By Christmas, in their final year things were getting very intense with finals looming. Pressure to achieve was mounting, albeit interspersed by ever more extravagant parties to mark the dawn of their twenty-first birthdays. Large family estates were lavishly prepared, yachts cleaned and distant holiday islands booked, to accompany the river of champagne and mountain of canapés. Despite wider concerns about student debt, access to higher education and career prospects thereafter for many Oxford families keeping their treasured offspring at university was cheap compared with years of private education with figures of £30,000 per year common place. Still, all this investment did not come without its expectations, and for many students, the weight of family expectation was heavy. Many knew that without a first their life plans would crumble and the thought of anything less than a 2:1 was inconceivable and would be a disaster.

For Hayley and Conrad their respective career paths seemed destined to coincide nicely, with Conrad working for his government on environmental policy development and Hayley based in Brussels, working as a translator for a large firm with extensive contracts to facilitate a range of international conferences all over the world. They planned to marry soon after graduation and establish a base in Stockholm.

Arabella planned to use her anticipated degree in English to forge a career in media and fashion. Her good looks, charm, not to mention wealth and her determination to succeed, all seemed to point to success. As regards to her relationship with Ahmed, she hoped to maintain links for clandestine lovemaking at every opportunity. She had secret visions of being whisked off on a white horse to ride bareback wearing pure white cloth to some romantic desert retreat.

Ahmed shared some thoughts with her but also had a

deeply private side. PPE would no doubt assist his career in government and diplomacy on behalf of the Arab world, and he felt more than ready to rejoin it.

Crichton had an interview the following day for the civil service fast track graduate scheme.

'Crichton, don't panic, you'll be fine. You can be a bit of a fool sometimes but remember, you are a very able scholar. That sharp intellect is rare and of course there is always father's influence,' said Conrad trying to be reassuring.

'I can't rely on father for this one, Conrad, he won't be at the interview! Will they ask me about ethical morality, or state security, homelessness, international trade or terrorism?'

'Possibly all of those, but you know the form. You've passed several stages already to get this far, so just be yourself. You've got career civil servant written all over you.'

Travelling down to London on the coach service known as the Oxford Tube, Crichton practised possible answers to likely questions, shuffled his notes and application form but most of all he was worried that his brief association with green politics may have already scuppered his chances.

The interview went well, he thought, and sure enough he was offered a place on the graduate scheme. All he had to do now was secure a 2:1 or above. Ruth was also pleased for him; in fact, for both of them, as she had already secured her place in financial services in London.

Pressure mounted as finals loomed and the workload intensified. This was the point where family investment, aspirations and ambitions met reality and the stakes were high. For Hayley ironically, despite her relative disadvantage many of these pressures didn't apply. Her family really had very little understanding and no expectations. She felt quite liberated, independent and relaxed, although she knew that if she failed there would be no family safety net. Generally, however, her situation tended to motivate rather than hinder her aspirations.

The Crown helped preserve their sanity and the friends all managed to hold it together to complete their finals. After the euphoria of the last exam, the traditional 'trashing' with water and food followed and the boost to the local dry-cleaning trade with the arrival of all the strict paraphernalia of formal dress known as Subfusc. The ending of the exams also brought a sharp sense of anti-climax, although for the friends this didn't last long before they moved seamlessly into party mode to celebrate their achievements, whatever they turned out to be. This was interspersed with the inevitable tension of waiting for results and the confirmation or destruction of life plans.

Fortunately, the period of waiting at Oxford was short and results were soon announced together with the details of the graduation ceremonies. The results were displayed as follows:

Arabella Taylor-Shaw – 2:2 in English.
Ruth Patel – first in Mathematics.
Hayley Smith – 2:1 in Modern Languages.
Crichton Broadhampton-Scott – 2:1 in History & Classics.
Conrad Lindstrand – first in Biology.
Ahmed Salib – 2:1 in PPE.

A good set of results were secured and the gate opened to their respective future career paths. More celebrations followed reflections on their Oxford experience and time to cement or conclude current relationships.

On the surface, Arabella was cool and realistic in those final days with Ahmed, knowing that he would return to Saudi Arabia and their contact would be overseen and limited. It was Ahmed who was more upset by the impending forced separation as he vowed to stay in touch forever, as she smiled politely while thinking of other encounters to come.

Ruth had long since secured her future with Crichton and the respective families had all the necessary arrangements in hand for an extravagant family wedding with no expense spared. A modest five-bedroom family home had been acquired in the Home Counties and was being refitted for their use, although initially it was likely that they would spend more time in their flat in London overlooking the Thames.

Hayley and Conrad enjoyed their remaining time in Oxford, full of love, expectation and dreams before embarking on their future life together. Their wedding was planned to be a relatively modest but tasteful affair, as a statement of love and commitment. Respective career paths were to intermingle over the years and their relationship seemed destined to deepen and grow stronger. Hayley's family still didn't really understand and her dad had tried to reassure her that 'if all this didn't work out', he felt sure that he could still get her the job back in the café with all its future prospects.

Ahmed's family kept the house in Jericho for future reference and made arrangements to let it out without delay. New groups of students would fill its rooms with the prospect of fulfilling their own ambitions.

In the final few days mixed feelings of pride, achievement, sadness and trepidation all intensified. When it came to the final evening in The Crown, it was actually quite a subdued affair. Good wishes were exchanged and promises made to keep in touch.

'I hope we do manage to maintain contact. A reunion in so many years' time would be really fun, to see what actually happened to us all that is!' exclaimed Ruth.

'Yes, we could all be anywhere in the world by then,' added Hayley with a sense of excitement.

Good-hearted conversation continued with exchanges of favourite memories and shared experiences. Crichton looked across at Ahmed and noticed that he looked quite detached.

'Ahmed,' he said, 'you are very quiet. What are you thinking?'

'Yes, I'm sorry. I suppose I'm feeling quite sad. Whilst

I'm looking forward to going home, for me there is much more of a sense of leaving, given the distance I'll be away from you all. It actually feels quite final.'

There was an uncomfortable silence as a tearful Arabella looked away, fearful that he may be right.

***

Finally, when the moment came to leave Oxford all had been said, all contact details shared and all promises made as they embarked on the next stage of their lives.

Chapter Eight

London, several years later

Sitting at his desk reading briefing papers, Crichton glanced up at his screen and noticed an email from Ahmed. It read:

Transferred to state security overseeing international relations, how are you?

Ahmed

Crichton worked in the middle echelons of power in the Home Office reporting to various senior people including ministers. The papers on his desk ranged from issues of domestic violence, honour killings and redefining dangerous dogs, to sex trafficking and modern slavery. He was busy. A moment's self-indulgence took him back to his beloved Oxford, the atmosphere, the history, the great classic buildings, The Crown pub and to old friends. He and Ruth were married and still together; she was expecting their second child imminently. He felt confident about the paternity of the first but wasn't so sure about the second, other than it would be loved whatever. The ringing of the internal phone brought him back to reality with a sudden order for his attendance at yet another meeting. Ahmed would have to wait.

The meeting was called to review progress with emergency planning in the event of a terrorist attack. It was widely attended by intelligence and security representatives including an American diplomat and several senior police officers, civil servants and junior politicians. It was chaired by the Minister. Various scenarios were discussed and contingency plans updated before coffee offered the opportunity of a welcome break and more informal exchanges.

'So how are you and Ruth these days, Crichton?' asked

one of the police officers.

'Fine, second child on the way,' he replied, briefly wondering if he was talking to its father, then immediately dismissed the thought.

'We really must meet for lunch again, I suggest my club, Crichton. You were a Canterbury man I remember?'

'Yes, correct and that would be nice.' The Assistant Chief Constable had studied Law and Ethics at Cambridge.

The meeting reconvened and continued in the same dire vein until lunch. Crichton caught the eye of the American diplomat as he headed off to his favourite burger bar.

'Things OK over the pond?' asked Crichton.

'Yes, I should say so, Anglo-American relations good as ever and no immediate threats really concern me.'

It was the next day that the bomb struck. A dirty bomb exploded in Times Square New York, instantly killing thirty people and seriously hampering the rescue effort. The immediate intelligence assessment pointed to ISIS involvement.

Efforts to build an intelligence picture had continued since their Oxford days and better international connections and cooperation were developing all the time, but no system of intelligence claimed to be perfect and this attack was not anticipated. Given the relatively modest scale of the attack it seemed likely that this was a mere 'trail run' with the real fear and prospect of a much larger follow-up attack to come that realistically could target any city in the Western world. This sent a cold shiver through the Western intelligence community.

Yemen

'Reports show a successful operation,' reported Jan.

'Good and plans for the follow-up?' asked Tak.

'Indications are that the Americans anticipate a further attack, so we have achieved our aim. Let them sweat!'

'Excellent!' concluded Tak.

There were prayers and celebrations.

London

Ahmed,

I got your email congratulations. Maybe together we can still save the world!

Keep in touch.

Crichton

Ahmed had strong loyalties to Arab interests but did not always see those interests to be at odds with Western aspirations. At times he was able to collect low level information and found ways to share it with Crichton.

This was useful and helped raise his profile as Crichton found subtle ways to reciprocate. The arrangement was mutually beneficial and sustainable.

It also attracted some interest from British and American intelligence agencies and their counterparts across the world.

Stockholm

Conrad and Hayley were both doing well and enjoying life. They kept their relationship fresh by enjoying short intensive bouts of togetherness interspersed with longer periods of separation, as their career paths converged and diverged as they travelled across Northern Europe and Scandinavia. They often reflected back to their time at Oxford and how random life could be to bring together two people from such diverse backgrounds who found themselves devoted to each other. Hayley also laughed to herself about how life could have turned out if she had stayed in Leeds, with such limited working prospects in her field. Whenever times were tough she just thought of working in that dreadful café. They often thought of their friends from Oxford and wondered how life had turned out for them and promised to make contact.

Conrad's specific responsibilities centred on research into sustainable forestation, the consequent impact on air quality, and reduction in risk of soil erosion. He had also worked on safety issues in the food chain, desalination, fish stock conservation and enhanced GM food production. He had gone on to further his studies at Stockholm University, securing both an MA and PHD. Conrad was now established as a leading expert in his field and was often consulted by a wide range of organisations, both governmental and commercial. He enjoyed the stimulation but most of all Conrad enjoyed the sense of satisfaction in believing he was making a difference and in a small way, fulfilling his Oxford aspirations.

Chapter Nine

New York

Brad returned from his enforced leave more angry and confused than refreshed. Did Chas really think that he was losing it? Why hadn't he listened to him? No answers seemed convincing, as negative thoughts mulled over in his mind. For the first time Brad felt quite uneasy about the job. He entered his office building, approached the lift and pushed the call button. Was this truly his vocation after all? Quickly trying to push such thoughts away, he walked into the lift and read the array of corporate messages and safety instructions, while he rose to the fourteenth floor.

When he reached the fourteenth floor, the lift door opened inviting him to move out into the corridor. Reluctantly, he did so pausing at the gents, but recognising it only as a delaying tactic he strode to the reception desk to satisfy security of his legitimacy. After the predictable banter about nothing of any importance, Brad made his way to his office still feeling uneasy. His desk was how he had left it and the office was alive with the familiar buzz of activity, anticipation and the smell of fresh coffee.

A tall African-American man approached him wearing a welcoming smile and extending his arm to offer a traditional handshake.

'Hi, I'm George. I replaced Chas, welcome back.'

'Hi, I'm Brad. So where's Chas?'

'Gone.'

'OK,' said Brad speculating.

'I've been reading some of your stuff, Brad, it's good. It makes sense to me. Fix yourself a coffee and let's talk about it when you are ready.'

Brad was both surprised and relieved and thought it best not to ask any more about Chas, and just to move on. *The moment is now*, he thought to himself trying to be reassuring.

Reinstalled, Brad Maier dusted off his desk and with it any self-doubt, grabbed a coffee and walked with confidence into the next office to address George.

'Brad, sit down. Good break I assume,' he said and without pausing continued. 'More sources tend to confirm your analysis that something is brewing. Reports from agents and contacts in East Asia suggest a number of terrorist fringe groups that may or may not be working together are building their supplies and recruiting networks.'

'What do we anticipate is the target?' asked Brad.

'Ah, that's the question, always the question, Brad. As you well know, intelligence is always incomplete and the skill is to bridge the gaps without paranoia, panic or political convenience. In this case the lead hunch is that an ISIS move is due east of Afghanistan towards China. Where and when precisely is still unknown.'

'And for what purpose, George?' asked Brad, sharp and keen as ever.

'It's unclear, Brad, but probably for territory and influence. Imagine if an ISIS group could link up with political dissatisfaction in Indo-China, what a potential power block that could be?'

'Yes… chilling,' replied Brad.

'Precisely. I have a dossier of reports for you to go through and I want your analysis on my desk in the morning. Good to have you back by the way, I'm told you are a good operator.' With that George smiled, handed Brad the dossier and left. With a mixture of excitement, dread and bemusement, Brad felt that he was back. He gathered up the dossier and got to work.

Yemen

Tak and Jan were making the most of the opportunity to capitalise on the chaos in Yemen and instigating various scams and schemes to further embarrass the government and extract money from the wealthy. Many of whom were only too glad to spend their cash on any thin hope of extracting themselves from the mess and instability that was leading predictably to the breakdown of civil order.

The country was in chaos leading to an unhealthy scramble to get out, with inevitably the rich and powerful leading the way. Many influential families had powerful allies in other neighbouring countries, but they too were in chaos leaving agonising decisions over what to do for the best; to stay or to go, to fight or to capitulate? Sadly for them, such panic was readily seized upon by criminal gangs to exploit their vulnerability.

Kuwait

A group made up of dissidents, remnants left over from the invasion by Iraq and more recent fundamentalist fighters viewed the ground from their well-established base. They had been tasked with making initial plans to extract money by bribery and by threatening the integrity of the water supply in the Middle East.

'You can sell oil, but you can't drink it. Without water wealth is nothing,' proclaimed the leader. 'This is an opportunity to create a distraction for the forces of the state while we recruit more brothers to our cause for the real fight against Western imperialism. The funds we extract will fill our coffers for the great battles to come.'

HMP Fulton Bank, North London

Fulton Bank was one of the new generation of private prisons built on an industrial scale to warehouse large numbers of offenders. It offered little more than containment to satisfy the perceived public will for deterrence and the political obsession with punishment.

Fulton Bank was the first British prison to combine male and female facilities in the same 'titan jail'. Separate arrangements applied to all functions, or so the authorities believed, within the large complex of buildings offering economies of scale.

Contained in her cell, Hilary Jameson sat calmly, now well established into her sentence keeping up with the news and green affairs as far as she could within the pathetic attempts by the authorities to restrict her access to information from the green extreme fringe. Realistically, she knew that she had no chance of escape – not yet at least – whilst still in relatively high security conditions. But she was patient, and took the long-term view that change was inevitable and was coming.

Hilary had limited contact with male prisoners of similar radical green persuasion by various means largely undetected by the authorities. Most of the prison concentration on combating 'radicalisation' such as it was, fell on the male estate whilst Hilary was making good ground recruiting women who were often perceived to be less of a threat. New 'recruits' came in various forms, not all needed to be of Eastern or Muslim extraction or tasked as potential suicide bombers, as influence could be so much more subtle. She found that staff too could be susceptible to persuasion. Wages and morale were low and there would always be those who were tempted to step outside their roles in order to line their own pockets. Identifying those under financial stress was easy. The vulnerable, the greedy and the immoral were tracked waiting for the right opportunity to offer to ease their burden. Some were fool enough to take it, despite the risks if the rewards were substantial enough and prisoners were pretty adept at identifying and exploiting their weakness.

Prison proved to offer an excellent recruiting ground for almost any scam, scheme or wildcat idea that promised the prospect of excitement, wealth and one in the eye for the system. Prisoners, already disenchanted, feeling marginalised and ignored, cynical about the system and general pissed off with their lot, were eager to engage and some of those would be potentially useful at some point in the future. Time after all was on their side.

Chapter Ten

London

Crichton Broadhampton-Scott had found that doors had continued to open for him, as they had all his life. He had progressed up the career ladder to a more senior position in the Home Office and was being vetted for further promotion. The official waiting to interview him had unrestricted access to his history and personal details in order to make an assessment of his loyalty, commitment and suitability to be party to the higher echelons of state security and to uncover any skeletons that may have made him vulnerable.

'Tell me, Mr Broadhampton-Scott, or are you OK with first names, is there anything that you are aware of that could potentially be an obstacle to your further promotion?'

Surprised by his directness Crichton stumbled into a hasty reply: 'No, no I don't think so. My father is a senior civil servant that may be regarded as suspect by some people I suppose?'

'Nepotism, yes we can counter that, anything else?' asked the official.

'Well, I suppose you know I'm gay?'

'Yes, it's not such an issue these days; public revelation isn't the shock horror that it used to be. Could you cope with exposure if it happened?'

'Yes, I think so,' said Crichton. 'It wouldn't be a surprise to anyone who is dear to me.'

'Senior responsibility brings with it extraordinary pressures sometimes and really tough dilemmas. How are you at taking tough decisions, Crichton?'

'I haven't got this far without having ruffled a few feathers.'

'We are not talking ruffling feathers here, Crichton, we are talking people being openly hostile and some of those wanting to kill you.'

'Yes, yes of course I understand and accept that.'

'And the potential impact on your family that goes with it?' asked the official.

His phone rang and Crichton took the call before the interview came to an end and the official calmly made no comment on his performance as he left. Crichton wondered whether he had done enough to satisfy the man, let alone the likely inquisition from Ruth later who he knew was very keen to see him promoted. He did so welcome her support, especially as she had been so busy recently and had effectively sacrificed her own career in the city for the sake of the children. Selfless she was, selfless. He admired her for that, he thought. She even had time to partake in good causes, which had taken her away for short periods of time. That was why she had insisted on the children being placed in a nursery, which was also designed for their own good in developing confidence and independence.

Saudi Arabia

Ahmed's life had moved on too. The anticipated perfect wife had been found for him, along with the senior status and role that he had expected. Ahmed recognised the privilege of his circumstances but still harboured some regrets that he could not have followed his heart and stayed with Arabella. He often thought of her and occasionally did meet for short periods of intense covert lovemaking, but it was never enough.

His position in the upper echelons of Saudi society and state security brought him the challenge he had craved for as a student. He felt comfortable pursuing the interests of the Arab world and resisting the West's assumptions of supremacy. His experiences of Oxford had not left him however. Being regarded as an *alien* he had been the immediate suspect in the police investigation over the Cornwall poisoning. The incident helped to remind him of who he truly was and of his loyalties and allegiance to Arab interests. Nevertheless, Ahmed was a realist and knew that he still had to work with the West. It was essential not to burn bridges but to maintain alliances where possible with those who may prove useful to him. Crichton and Conrad were two such people in his eyes.

The unfolding security situation troubled him. ISIS had taken significant areas of territory across North Africa and the Middle East, including their latest acquisition of substantial parts of Jordan. Smaller Arab states looked to Saudi Arabia for leadership and protection and he sensed that his countrymen were soon to be tested. He worried that ISIS may focus on extending their influence further east and look to China as a source of support. He knew that the Chinese would resist, at least officially but in reality was not sure if it suited them to use ISIS to destabilise the West and thus bolster their own position.

An international conference was imminent to discuss some of these issues as well as global resource security. He wondered whether Crichton or Conrad would attend and rather hoped that they would.

Turkey, the international conference

Ahmed took his place as one of the delegates in the great hall, which dated back to the Ottoman Empire. As he looked around he nodded gently at those he recognised from his dealings in international affairs. He was looking forward to the opening address, which was heralded to be both controversial and challenging. Ahmed opened his programme and read the opening brief introducing the initial presenter who was to address global security in the light of climate change, over population and growing shortages of both food and water. As he read on, Ahmed glanced at the name of the speaker: Professor Conrad Lindstrand from Sweden and graduate of Canterbury College Oxford.

Conrad, now a senior academic and government policy advisor as well as Chair and member of many organisations promoting environmental harmony, was talking to fellow guests as his wife Hayley briefed the contingent of interpreters. Hayley was looking forward to leading the group for the first time at such an important and high profile event. It was not unusual for them to be working on the same event but odd nonetheless, as despite their physical proximity on such occasions, they rarely saw each other. On this occasion, however, they were determined to find time to meet and spend some time together.

Conrad both renewed previous associations and made new acquaintances with consummate ease as he circulated around the reception area with a glass in hand. It was then that he noticed a tall delegate who was unmistakably English and began to wonder. Conrad enjoyed the stimulation of being with fellow academics, policy makers and thinkers, although he was not quite so comfortable with politicians. He really hoped that this time the conference would really result in some tangible change and not just another set of meaningless platitudes.

As Crichton Broadhampton-Scott attached his delegate name badge and turned around, he saw Conrad at a distance with a Dutch representative and immediately walked over to approach him.

'Conrad! My dear boy, how are you?'

'Crichton, you look so well and so well preserved if I may say so!'

'I saw your name on the delegate list and was so looking forward to seeing you. It sometimes feels like Oxford was only yesterday and other times in a different era altogether.'

'Yes, quite. Ruth OK? Any children yet?' asked Conrad.

'Oh yes of course, and you?'

'Too busy I'm afraid, but Hayley is here too, as an interpreter… you'll get to see her later.'

'Excellent! Have you noticed another familiar name?' Crichton asked, pointing out Ahmed Salib on the delegate list.

The conference got quickly underway and Conrad was duly invited to take the stage. He was able to offer an impassioned plea for world action before it really was too late. The reaction from the venerable audience was more than polite acknowledgement, but he knew full well that it would take far more than that to change the world for the better.

Conrad had outlined recent research and some critical trends and identified a number of priority areas for action. Critical amongst those were food production, water security and green energy. He made a compelling and heartfelt case for radical but achievable action as he progressed towards his concluding remarks.

'Fellow delegates, whilst the challenge is considerable and the challenge is now, the tragedy would be to ignore it when in fact it is within our grasp to make significant changes in sufficient time, to not only make a difference now, but more importantly, for future generations to come.

'In relation to food production, we must simply increase it and move on from the hysterical objection to genetically modified crops. We need to move away from the position where half the world is suffering from the ill effects of obesity and over indulgence whilst the other half starves. You do the maths, it is not difficult; *it is achievable*.

'In relation to water security, we must invest more research into economic and efficient desalination. We must radically redesign our approach to consumption, and aim to provide *all* across the *whole world* with access to clean drinking water by redirecting funds away from mutual self-destruction. It's not conceptually difficult and *it is achievable*.

'As regards green energy, all new buildings must aim to be energy self-sufficient via wind and solar power. As oil fields in the hot and arid parts of the world dry up, they must be replaced by new solar fields and therefore we must accelerate the rate of replacement of harmful fossil fuel engines in favour of renewable battery power. The technologies are already there – *it is achievable*.

'And finally, friends, and far more controversially, we must as a world community, as one, commit to rebalancing world resources to those who need them most. That is the only route to long-term security. Not only would that ultimately make economic and humanitarian sense, it is essential if the two current worlds of rich and poor are to coexist without descending into anarchy and chaos.'

With that Conrad sat down to widespread applause, which he hoped but somehow doubted was a reflection of commitment to act. There followed a range of speakers and sub groups to explore the major issues as the conference moved through the agenda.

It was not until well after dinner that Conrad and Crichton were finally joined by Ahmed, who had been called away to a separate briefing.

'Gentlemen, I'm so pleased to see you both here, and I do apologise for being so late,' said Ahmed, and immediately they started laughing.

'There's nothing new there then, Ahmed. Do you remember you were always late at Oxford?' said Crichton, laughing.

'Yes, sadly I do, and as you see nothing has changed. Anyway, a drink,' he said flamboyantly as he looked around for another champagne-bearing waiter. 'A toast… to old times.'

'To old times!' they all agreed.

After the customary and polite exchange of pleasantries, the three old friends talked more seriously about the conference and its important world agenda.

'Who would have thought all those years ago that we'd be sitting here like this now?' said Conrad, with Ahmed adopting a look of surprise.

'Wasn't it inevitable?' he countered.

They talked more of careers, aspirations and family over yet more champagne until the early hours, when finally Conrad broke the impasse and retired to bed. Just as Crichton was rising to do the same, Ahmed took his arm.

'Crichton, come with me into this side room, out of hearing,' he insisted. 'You realise we now have the power to influence this, don't you? We could actually stop this madness.' Ahmed gazed into his eyes with a piercing intensity before one of the staff interrupted to announce that the bar facilities were about to close. They returned to the main room, embarrassed to wonder what the innocent waiter may have made of their encounter before another delegate staggered over to them and started to bang on about the history of the UN. Eventually, they escaped his ranting and parted quickly to proceed to bed.

The following day the conference was alive with acclaim for Conrad's address and the world's media had announced the dawning of a new age of global cooperation to save the planet. Conrad was pleased with the response of course, but cautious nevertheless. He enjoyed a quiet breakfast with Crichton and learnt later that Ahmed had left early at his family's request to attend a dying relative.

Chapter Eleven

Saudi Arabia

Ahmed had returned from the conference early on the pretence of family business, only to find a different but equally distressing scene. A junior member of the government had been killed, timed to coincide with the conference to distract from its message and remind the world that the struggle for supremacy wasn't over. Was this terrorist action, ISIS, criminal gangs or powerful vested interest paying others to do their dirty work? The Saudi government had sufficient influence to delay any news coverage to complete an initial investigation, which pointed the finger firmly at the latter scenario. International business was keen to suggest in the public mind that tinkering with global politics would only unleash the unknown and that they would be better served to trust the status quo. The fact that ISIS would inevitably get the blame they reasoned wouldn't do them any harm either.

At the same time another force was at work, one which was far more threatening.

***

Two days later, Arabella called on their secret line. She had heard that there had been trouble and was concerned to establish that Ahmed was safe. He reassured her, but not himself. He still missed her terribly.

Ahmed's wife had planned a large gathering in their honour, which really only added to his feelings of regret. Later, together with their four children, they enjoyed a private reunion and polite celebration. Many guests appeared and many more would have gladly conspired to be able to attend. It was formal, and the rigidity and pretence at times, angered Ahmed. Sometimes he felt so trapped, so bound by duty and expectation.

Before the conference ended and the tragic news of the murder of the official was broadcast, Conrad and Crichton got to meet Hayley behind the scenes as she was winding up her operation. She was obviously delighted that her services had been effective and that she had been complimented. Conrad looked forward to returning to the relative peace of Sweden and of academic life after his moment in the spotlight. For Crichton it was lovely to see Hayley and he felt pleased that she and Conrad seemed so happy.

On his return, Crichton heard of rumours that it was the British authorities that had murdered the Saudi official in an attempt to discredit their security apparatus prior to bids to hold the next international conference there in preference to London. Unfortunately, the rumours – although rigorously denied of course – had also reached Saudi ears and were not well received.

British intelligence, however, was seriously concerned about the future of the Middle East. How long could the Saudi government resist the pressures from radical elements to reform and from radical extremists like ISIS, to endorse the new fundamentalism? Secretly, MI6 wanted a new inside man to unpick some of these developments and forewarn them of any likely change of direction by the Saudis, or of any likely serious threat to their power base.

After Ahmed's secret comments at the end of the conference, Crichton was not entirely sure what Ahmed had meant about them collectively stopping 'this madness'? At least, that is what he had remembered Ahmed saying. Which *we*? Which *madness*, and stop *what* exactly? he thought.

Over the coming months, Ahmed and Crichton found new ways to exchange information, concerns and trends that amounted to low level intelligence. The question remained, however, whether they held enough confidence in each other to believe the information and sustain the link? If he was honest, Crichton was not sure and thought that Ahmed probably felt the same.

It was not long before the visit came. Crichton always remembered the visit by several officials who confirmed that he had been approved for further promotion but that the appointment was conditional. Conditional upon him agreeing to pass low level intelligence to the Saudi regime via his established link with Ahmed in order to gain his trust for possible future exploitation, the nature of which of course being unspecified. Initially, Crichton felt affronted to think that these men had regarded his honour so cheaply. He was given twenty-four hours to decide. It proved to be a long night and a difficult decision. *How good are you at tough decisions, Crichton?* he remembered them asking him at the assessment. He was unsure who – if anyone – he could share this burden with. Such was the nature of his work it was impossible to know who else in the organisation would be aware of this, and of course, the official protocol was to say nothing to anyone in such circumstances.

Later that evening whilst in bed, Ruth sensed his unease. He tried to explain what he wasn't allowed to say, and informed her that he had to make a difficult decision. Ruth calmly and helpfully reassured him to trust his judgement and to ensure that the right people knew of his loyalty. He slept a little easier as a result.

Chapter Twelve

American intelligence indications were in fact correct that a new front was about to open with ISIS launching attacks beyond Afghanistan and Pakistan into Chinese territory. Partly funded by the Russians, it also suited the Chinese to covertly allow ISIS to make some ground early on and deal with some dissident groups on their behalf with a brutality that even the Chinese would have baulked at.

Despite some anticipation, the move when it did come took the West by surprise. Wrong footed and lacking a political consensus, the West assumed its usual posture of much debate and little action. This was of course precisely what the ISIS planners had assumed and whilst lofty protestations prevailed, they rolled on further into Chinese territory.

***

China had developed a complex of thousands of dams to store water on a massive scale in an attempt to ensure their own water security. Shifting priority from coal to hydro-electric power was also a shrewd move, at least on their part. The downside, however, was the inevitable impact further down the river in Tibet, Vietnam, Cambodia and Bangladesh. Twenty-two million Chinese citizens had already been relocated since the 1950s, to accommodate hydro-electric power schemes and a further million Tibetans since 1990. These new arrangements represented a major shift in power in favour of the Chinese, leaving the other countries connected by the same river systems highly vulnerable to disruption in water levels. Not only would this affect access to drinking water, but it would have an adverse impact on both agriculture and fisheries.

As the Western intelligence agencies tracked ISIS' progress and briefed their respective governments, concern was mounting. Some limited success had been achieved in

North Africa in returning for example Egypt back to some level of stability, but ISIS were still a significant threat to both world order and stability. This new dimension in China was, however, of a different order given the variety of interests at stake.

New York

Brad and George sat in their office considering the implications.

'You know, Brad, I sense a Russian hand in this, which embarrasses us and threatens notions of Western supremacy. In addition, it compromises China as the predicted next world power to emerge, following domination by the USA.'

'Um, you mean they actually support it?' asked Brad.

'I mean they probably suggested it, planned it and are funding it, Brad.'

'What's your take on the mood from the White House?'

'Difficult to judge, but the President is not keen on military action, that's for sure,' said George.

'What, fear of getting embroiled in another foreign war with little purpose, aim or direction?' asked Brad.

'Yes, and getting an extremely large bill for it.'

'And what do the Brits think, George?'

'The Prime Minister is sounding tough, but I suspect there's little enthusiasm for action there either.'

'So what's our stance, George?'

'We watch, we monitor and we wait, Brad.'

***

Two months later, Brad had compiled a file of intelligence that amounted to a pattern of minor demands from terrorist groups being sent to different Western governments. He had been watching the trend and judged that it was time to discuss it with George.

'Hi, Brad, you wanted to discuss a development with

me? Sit down, what's on your mind?'

'George, it might be nothing but instinct tells me that this could be a problem. I've picked up a growing pattern of demands from different terrorist sub groups aimed at various Western governments.'

'We're talking Islamic fundamentalist groups, Brad?'

'Yes, of course. My guess is that they are trying to tease out the West's response to this tactic. We know that whilst officially most Western governments claim not to negotiate with terrorists for fear of simply encouraging greater demand, in reality it happens all the time. Are they testing our resolve?'

'Could be, but you can't assume coordination here; it maybe that they don't know anything much about the actions of other similar groups.'

'Yes, I accept that, George, but I'm still concerned.'

'OK, Brad, keep me informed.'

London and Riyadh, Saudi Arabia

Via a secure unofficial telephone link, Ahmed was in conversation with Crichton.

'Crichton, I'm feeling very uncomfortable here recently. I fear instability.'

'Why, Ahmed, what's changed so suddenly?'

'No, it's not sudden, my friend, but the security situation here is deteriorating. The influence of ISIS both from within and outside is growing and I don't know who to trust anymore.'

'Have you got anything else for me today, Ahmed, apart from that?'

'Only that I fear for my safety and wonder how long I can stay here, my friend.'

Crichton was surprised and concerned by the apparent level of emotion in Ahmed's voice. He was at a loss as to how to respond before they lost the connection and the call ended prematurely. Crichton passed on the concerns as he did routinely to a secure post box for analysis and interpretation.

Two days later Ahmed was detained by Saudi internal security officials and driven at speed to a secret location. If Ahmed was concerned before, now he was terrified. How much did they know? Had his call been intercepted, he wondered. He didn't know but feared that soon he would have the answer to his question. He knew that loyalty was expected and that disloyalty would be punished.

Initially, his interview was calm and respectful, suggesting that he had not been discovered to have established a regular unofficial link with a foreign power. The room was tidy and well furnished, not suggesting a prison or interrogation centre. After some light opening questions, the emphasis suddenly changed to be more serious and intrusive. A more senior man entered the room and sat down opposite him with a file of papers.

'Ahmed, your loyalty is not in question. On the contrary, you are to be complimented for your initiative in nurturing your Oxford contacts to secure information that could prove useful in promoting Arab interests.'

Ahmed felt substantial relief if indeed that was how his questioner perceived the situation to be.

'I have here copies of certain transcripts that you would be aware of,' he said whilst laying the file containing some of his communications open on the table in front of him. 'Ahmed, we live in dangerous times and in such circumstances we all have to make sacrifices. We need you to cooperate more closely with our ISIS colleagues to ensure that Allah prevails and the infidels are punished. You will receive certain communications to feed to your infidel friend to ensure he is distracted and you will send them by your usual means. You will also continue to send some low level accurate intelligence to maintain his trust.'

Ahmed didn't consider that this was an invitation, and nodded in compliance.

'Oh, and, Ahmed, don't have any thoughts of sharing this development with him. You have your family to consider. I assure you that you and they would suffer unimaginable consequences should you choose to disobey me.'

Ahmed was left in no doubt about the genuineness of the message or the messenger. Whichever way he looked at it, he considered that he really didn't have any choice but to comply. Options and consequences flashed through his mind as he was driven back to the centre of town and invited to return to his work. He was assured that details of the arrangement would be made clear to him soon enough.

As he walked away, Ahmed felt uncertain as to his loyalty to the Saudi regime. Surely it was inconceivable for him to believe that the Saudi state could be in any way connected to ISIS.

Over the coming days and weeks, Ahmed wrestled with his conscience about how he could maintain any dignity and self-respect. If he was to act as a means to mislead not only a friend but potentially the West, it was likely Crichton would become exposed or entrapped as a result. Whilst he was an Arab and had little respect for the West, if the choice was between the West and ISIS, then that was a very different matter and a much more complex dilemma.

Chapter Thirteen

Crichton continued to send low level intelligence to Ahmed, without any knowledge of his true position. Ahmed faithfully passed it on, not knowing of Crichton's link with official intelligence either, although he had wondered. This arrangement continued between friends for some time with little impact on the wider intelligence picture, whilst both sides hoped that the investment would prove to be worth it in the longer run.

Yemen

Members of a senior planning group assembled for a critical meeting. It had been decided that matters had progressed sufficiently to launch a new major terror initiative aimed at challenging and destabilising the West to a catastrophic degree. This was a proud moment. It was the culmination of many aspirations and represented more than a life's work to some of the participants. The belief was strong that this action could actually shift the balance of world power.

They proudly collated reports from different groups and areas to confirm a picture of their current position, both in terms of geographical dominance and local political influence or intimidation.

Many groups were represented from a wide spectrum of Islamic and criminal interest.

No names were used, no records kept, no secret recordings made as the group designed their dark plan. Feasibility was confirmed, configurations established and detailed tasks allocated.

New York and London

Brad and George still watched, still waited, ever vigilant, ever present. When and where would they strike, they speculated? They knew that the advance into China had been a success from an ISIS perspective, but indications were too vague and disparate about any potential moves thereafter.

George had always feared a technological strike aimed at disabling computer and IT systems, which were now of course mainstream and essential to almost all government and commercial enterprise. *If you really wanted to strike at the heart of Western power and supremacy, surely that was a high probability option,* he thought as he deployed his resources accordingly.

London intelligence was more concerned about the potential bomb threat and the threat from within from those vulnerable to radicalisation. Elements of the intelligence community – although not most politicians – recognised that somehow we had failed large elements of *new* Britain, who felt underprivileged, isolated and angry. An ideal combination if you were looking to recruit terrorists, whilst others just saw the threat and disregarded the cause.

'Radicalisation of the young cannot be healthy in a democratic society,' the minister had told them. Correspondence from his northern constituency often included communication from worried parents concerned about the possibility of young minds being twisted and incited to travel the route through Europe to Syria and across North Africa in the name of jihad, only to be abused, violated and often killed.

Other than building barriers at Dover, the more liberal dilemma for some politicians and clerics was how to combine a selective open door policy, aimed at welcoming and most importantly integrating foreign talent, whilst avoiding that potential isolation and resentment. Most agreed that as a small island, Britain had to be realistic about restricting immigration and be more discerning in identifying and barring criminal, terrorist or other destabilising elements from entry. But whilst we talked, we failed to act and allowed the potential for terrorist cells to develop.

In London, MI5 knew that they and their police

colleagues couldn't possibly identify and track all potential terrorists living across the UK. They could at best only speculate and prioritise who to target, knowing that any such process was always going to be imperfect and vulnerable to criticism from the hindsight brigade.

Meanwhile over in New York, there was a development.

'Brad, a minute of your time,' demanded George.

'I'm coming, George.'

'Right, something tangible, Brad. London tells us that a group of known activists have been caught by North Wales police, showing an unhealthy interest in certain reservoirs in their part of the world.'

'And their analysis?'

'It ties in with our own intelligence of a similar nature in several US states. It could be a rerun of the British Cornwall case, where water poisoning was used or a threat to the integrity of the dams themselves. After all, flooding can cause an awful mess, disruption and loss of life.'

'Yes, do we have a favoured scenario, George?'

'Yes, the thinking is more towards the Cornwall approach.'

'Are we sure, George?'

'No, but that's what we are instructed to go with. We have political approval at top level from both sides of the pond.'

Chapter Fourteen

Hilary Jameson had become unwell and her condition was deteriorating, causing both her and the prison authorities serious concern, albeit for different reasons. In the Governor's office, senior staff shared information and discussed issues of the day, as per their usual morning meetings.

'Governor, I have to report concern from the medical staff again about Jameson. They are getting really jumpy that they can no longer justify not referring her to outside consultation, at least on medical grounds.'

'Um… and security?'

'Sir, you know our view.'

'Yes and I agree. Jameson is not the sort of prisoner you let out… even on medical escort; in my view, even if she is dying, but the bleeding heart brigade wouldn't agree. I think I need to take advice on this one, if only to cover my own arse.'

'Very wise, Sir,' the Deputy Governor agreed.

Later the Governor made the call to the Area Manager.

'Alistair, it's Mark here, I have a situation that I'd like your view on.'

'Yes, go on.'

'Remember the Cornwall water poisoning case? Hilary Jameson, green fanatic was convicted. Well, we hold her here and generally I feel we are on top of the security and intelligence battle. However, the medical people tell me that she is seriously ill and they are duty bound to refer her to an outside hospital to confirm a diagnosis and consider treatment. The reality is that if we let her go, albeit by escort, the risk of escape is magnified.'

'Yes, I see,' considered the Area Manager. 'Mark, I'll run it past our legal people first and it might have to go right up to the minister. But the implications are obvious if it goes horribly wrong. If it becomes a regular pattern, then I agree, the green brigade would almost certainly have a go. Leave it with me.'

The Governor was satisfied that he had taken the matter off his shoulders and felt confident that now it would rumble on indefinitely with no one being prepared to make a decision, leaving him to manage the prison with his own arse covered. He smiled to himself before going to talk to the medics.

Prisoners came under general NHS provision and were no longer treated directly by prison staff. This was not a development that he had welcomed at the time and one that, as he had predicted, had caused many a conflict of interest. He had always stuck to the view that it would be easier to defend a case of denial of outside treatment than one of escape of a known dangerous offender, both to the public whom he still considered he served and to the political establishment.

As he approached the medical unit, he knew that they would take a different view.

The senior nurse on duty was an efficient and principled woman, but someone that he felt that he could talk to openly.

'Sani, Hilary Jameson. I've put the case to the AM and he's promised to get back to me, but don't expect an answer quickly. If she goes out at all it will be cuffed and with a double escort.'

'OK,' said Sani. 'Well, you know what I think about women and use of cuffs on medical escort, but I accept that in this case the security implications are unusual. Medically speaking, our view is that the condition is genuine and is life threatening and that on that basis alone, we cannot justify denying her access to medical treatment that we can't provide here. She has to go out.'

'Yes. OK, Sani, that's what I expected that you would say, but it's with Alistair now and we will have to wait for his approval. In the meantime, manage her as best you can.'

'And if she dies?'

'Then she dies. We all die eventually,' he replied starkly.

Green activists knew of her situation and they knew the

law and the medical protocols. They anticipated procrastination but were confident that eventually authority would be granted for a medical escort and they set about lobbying for the same to anyone and everyone who had an interest.

***

Months passed and Hilary's condition deteriorated whilst deliberations continued. Eventually, the Area Manager was in a position to reply to the Governor.

'Mark, it's Alistair re Jameson, the decision is that she goes out for a diagnosis only in the hope that it's not as serious as your medics assume and that adequate treatment can be offered within a secure environment.'

'OK, Sir, your call and the precise security arrangements are with me?'

'Yes, obviously, Mark, use of cuffs, etc. and normal coordination with the police and so on... the times and details have to be strictly secured and only known by the smallest possible group.'

'OK, Sir, I'll make the arrangements.'

The medical staff were pleased and in a brief meeting between Sani, Sue the head of Security and the Governor, it was agreed to reassure Jameson. However, it was decided not to tell her the precise details, until she was in the car and on the way in order to keep knowledge of the facts as tight as possible. Sue briefed the local police and the prison police liaison officer and a medical referral was made for a consultation with a prisoner who was not named.

The hospital had recently appointed a temporary admin assistant to deal with hospital appointments in the cardiology unit. She waited for the referral knowing that her role would be vital in feeding the information to Hilary's friends outside. She knew enough about the condition, the timing and the source of the referral, to ascertain who was being referred without the need for names. The referral was made. The date kept closely guarded by the prison, leaked by the carefully planted appointments secretary and the next stage of the plan was implemented.

Two days before the appointment was due and the date finally sanctioned, a disturbance broke out in the male part of the large prison. In haste to gain efficiency savings the security department for the whole prison had been merged and for those two days was totally absorbed in dealing with the male disturbance. In thirty-six hours, it was brought under control swiftly and efficiently, resulting in much back slapping and self-congratulations. Unfortunately, during the excitement, the message that should have gone to the local police to inform them that the expected escort was to take place the following day was overlooked and was never sent.

Consequently, when the two experienced and confident officers escorted Ms Jameson out of the prison and into a waiting taxi, they assumed that the police and no one else were aware of their intentions.

As the taxi approached the hospital, the officers informed the prisoner of the purpose of her escort. They pulled up at some traffic lights in the middle lane correctly aligned for the next leg of the journey. Two cars pulled up alongside them on either side and with military efficiency one secured the side doors of the taxi from the inside lane. From the outside lane, two men quickly got out and opened the side door of the vehicle, showed the officers a machete and threatened to cut the cuffs, with or without their limbs still attached unless there were unlocked. Given the limited options the officers complied and Hilary Jameson – enemy of the state – was neatly transferred into the waiting car in the outside line and sped off to freedom.

Chapter Fifteen

There were some very embarrassed people facing some very tricky questions. The media blew the incident out of all proportion and politicians with no real experience of anything at all, claimed that they would have done better and postulated how anyone in their right mind could have possibly authorised this escort. The story rumbled on for a week or so but in time after the customary public reassurance statement and consequential tightening of prison procedures, the hype calmed down. Nevertheless, it had been a serious lapse of security, leaving Jameson still at large.

The police for their part could quite rightly state that this wasn't their failing and that they would do their best to apprehend the prisoner. With political expediency, significant resources were deployed trying to track her down, establish the true identity of the temporary appointments secretary and anyone else involved, but all had gone to ground. The taxi driver's statement confirmed that the snatch appeared to have been well planned, was efficiently executed, and in the circumstances the officers had no choice but to comply with their instructions and unlock the cuffs. It had all happened so quickly that no useful identification was established of the assailants and no one came forward who might have been on that road at that time to assist further. In other words, the investigation drew a blank, leaving any thoughts about who was responsible to be nothing more than pure speculation.

In the intelligence community, the concern centred round how much influence or expertise Hilary Jameson might add to the green extreme fringe and increase the risk of a terrorist attack. They had to conclude that the mere availability of Jameson alone added weight to the likelihood of the water poisoning scenario.

New York

George was keen to receive whatever conclusions had come out of the British investigation, as well as offer his sympathies to those involved, including the prison officers whose welfare was all but forgotten in the aftermath. Clearly, George was disappointed by the lack of information available both about the details of the escape and the whereabouts of Hilary Jameson, but managed not to further embarrass the British by saying so. He was due to review what was known and unknown with Brad.

'Morning, Brad,' said George enthusiastically. 'We need to have a look at what we've got.'

'Right, George. The latest incident report involves a suspected recce of a reservoir serving the Utah area. It could represent a threat to the dam or the water supply.'

'Was anyone arrested? Were they known players?'

'No,' said Brad, 'unfortunately, there were no arrests. The sightings were vague and from some distance away by a local farmer.'

'OK, I also have a report from France about sightings of small groups showing interest at night in certain hydroelectric sites in the Alps.'

'So, that's another angle to consider?' said Brad.

'Yes, seems so,' said George. 'Where will they strike, Brad, where will they strike?'

Cobra, London

In the light of recent concerns, a meeting had been convened to assess the current threat to the British water supply system.

'Morning everyone, I don't need to remind you all of the severity of this current threat, so let's crack on,' remarked the Prime Minister. 'Can we have the security summary please?'

'Yes, Sir. A direct threat was issued last night by a group

calling themselves "The Green Alliance", to poison both water and food supplies across Europe unless certain demands are met.'

'What is the nature of the demands?' asked the Prime Minister.

'Sir, there are a wide range of demands relating to broadly environmental issues, many of which would be difficult to achieve, let alone verify. And not quickly in any event.'

'Such as?'

'For example stop the loss of the polar ice cap.'

'Reducing the rate of decline hasn't been achieved yet. Are these people real?' asked the Prime Minister.

'The intelligence assessment is that at least in part, as these targets are set so high there is probably an acceptance that they are not achievable. Therefore, they want us to fail and for them to feel justified in carrying out their threats.'

The mood was sombre as the members took in the implications. After a short silence a senior member spoke up: 'We've been here before; you can't negotiate with people like this, it's a waste of time. Our only realistic strategy is to defeat them.'

The message was stark, but reluctantly accepted as realistic.

***

Later that week the Prime Minister was due to attend a European meeting of heads of state and intelligence representatives to assess the combined threat across the whole of Europe.

The French Minister outlined more details of their intelligence assessment and a similar picture emerged in both Italy and Spain. No one, however, had anticipated the threat to food supplies as well and this dominated much of the discussion.

'Can we be more precise about the threat to food?' posed the British Prime Minister.

'As I see it, it wouldn't be that difficult to infiltrate the food production chain at any number of points and compromise it with minimal chance of detection,' replied the French representative.

'You really think we are that vulnerable?'

'Yes, with the number of illegal immigrants entering Europe over recent years, the scope for planting "sleepers" is almost incalculable. Therefore, we must assume that people are already in place in farms, abattoirs, packing plants, sales and distribution across Europe, ready to strike if given the call.'

'What's the motivation?' asked the Prime Minister.

'To disable the West and increase the influence of Islamic fundamentalism.'

'So, this isn't about green politics at all then?'

'No, fundamentally this is about ISIS extending their influence and a number of interested powerful backers looking to reduce Western power and advance the rise of a new world order. The environmental aspect is just a means, not an end in itself, to use Green Terror as a weapon. At least that's how we think ISIS see it. Genuine green groups, however, have a different agenda.'

This was chilling news to those present, who had started to digest some of the implications. If both food and water were under threat, then this was a threat of almost unprecedented magnitude.

After a considerable pause, the MI6 representative posed a further question: 'Prime Minister, there is another issue that we really must address.'

'Go on,' he said.

'The Chinese question, Sir. Given the reports that suggest an intention for ISIS to move into China; in fact, that has already started to some degree. We need to ask why? If the ultimate target is to threaten the Chinese dam system, then what we have just discussed becomes a side issue. The scale of the potential consequences across East Asia of poisoning the water supply would be beyond catastrophic.'

'Yes, I see, and what do you suggest.'

'Sir, I think we need some local eyes and ears on the ground.'

'And how do you suggest that we do that?'

'Special forces involvement is the obvious starting point, Prime Minister.'

'Have you discussed this with them yet?'

'No, Sir.'

'Very tricky I must say,' said the Prime Minister. 'We really don't want to risk upsetting the Chinese. We have no legitimacy there and we've got more than enough enemies to contend with as it is, thank you very much.' He turned to the Head of the Armed Services: 'General, what are your initial thoughts?'

'Anything is possible, Prime Minister, but covert boots on the ground, covering such vast distances with minimal support would be challenging to say the least.'

'Um, the political implications are considerable too. It would have to be a deniable operation but usual cover stories about being lost out of area whilst on exercise won't wash here. How could we possibly justify operating that far out of our influence, and wouldn't our soldiers stick out like a sore thumb anyway? They simply couldn't wander about the Chinese countryside armed in uniform, and expect to remain unnoticed, could they, General?'

'Well, in essence, that is what they do... but you do have a point, Sir. I'd need time to consider it. Perhaps the use of Ghurkha troops would be a possibility, to blend into the local population. Sometimes you just have a take a different approach.'

'OK, or we could simply leave well alone and concentrate on looking after our own backyard. Anyway, can you give it some thought, Sir James, and report back promptly in the event that we may have to countenance this,' the PM concluded as the members dispersed.

Chapter Sixteen

Saudi Arabia

Ahmed was busy in his new enhanced role, gathering information, making plans, enhancing Arab interests and laying a false briefing trial for his friend Crichton back in the UK. Crichton of course was responding in kind and both intelligence services seemed satisfied with their respective positions.

One of the strands of false information Ahmed was feeding Crichton was to over-emphasise the significance of the expansion into Chinese territory. This in fact was far more tentative than substantial in the hope of gaining support from the Chinese and not antagonising them. It was, however, a distraction from the main event taking place across Europe.

Despite reassurance from his family that his role was an honourable one, Ahmed still felt a sense of mixed loyalties as he went about his business. He was careful not to arouse any suspicion from those who he knew were monitoring his every move and would strike without mercy if they felt it necessary. Arabella on the other hand offered reassurance of a different kind, hope of a new life, if that was ever realistic. Questions about his true conscience ran through his troubled mind.

London

Crichton dutifully passed on Ahmed's communications as instructed to the allocated secure post box, whilst maintaining a healthy scepticism about their worth. In the final analysis, the question he kept asking himself was, 'Do I really trust him?' Crichton received little feedback about this aspect of his work other than occasional polite nods from those in the know. He did wonder how long he would be required to maintain this uneasy alliance. Adding to his misgivings of course was the fact that he couldn't share his feelings with anyone. Ruth was intuitive enough to sense some of his unease but knew better than to question him; rather, she just offered vague reassurance that she was so proud of him and was sure he'd do the right thing, which was at least some comfort.

Occasional communication with Conrad helped and although no details were exchanged, their continued friendship was a genuine source of support. Conrad too had his difficulties to share in overcoming resistance to positive change. It just helped sometimes to hear a familiar voice away from any intrusion and to reflect back on their carefree and idealistic days at Oxford.

In response to Crichton's messages and other sources of intelligence the authorities across the Western world were starting to take sensible precautionary measures to add to food and water security and monitor a little more closely known players and arrest them where possible. Regular meetings were set up to share information and to start to prepare emergency and contingency plans. Food stocks were increased and to some extent water supplies with some water being able to be pumped to underground storage, was deemed to be less vulnerable to a terrorist attack.

There was an incident in Spain where three men were shot by the authorities in a botched attempt at breaking into a water supply and treatment centre. The authorities were pleased and sensed that it bought them some time in their dealings with the Green Alliance and sent out a clear message.

Western concern continued about ISIS and their intentions in China. Not unusually the Chinese authorities gave very little away in any international forums; nevertheless, there was suspicion that ISIS suited their wishes to purge certain disloyal elements in the western provinces of China and that they were happy to let it happen, whilst expressing notional international condem-nation.

Intelligence agencies were trying to make progress in establishing likely sources of poisons, their chemical makeup, manufacturing processes and likely distribution routes to be able to intercept them if necessary. Progress, however, was slow.

Other efforts went into producing mountains of false data to try to persuade the Green Alliance that real progress was being made towards their demands and that it was in their interests to be patient. Doubts existed about how successful this approach was likely to be, but the judgement was that it was worth trying.

Small inroads and successes were being registered with modest finds of poison stocks across Europe. There was always the thought that intelligence only led to the margins. Still, the authorities were reasonably satisfied with progress so far.

The following day the Head of the Armed Services reported back to the Prime Minister with some outline thoughts on how to infiltrate into China and gather some more direct intelligence.

'Prime Minister.'

'Sir James, come in and sit down. I understand that you have some information for me.'

'Yes, Sir. But first of all whilst this is not my jurisdiction, I wanted to clarify what diplomatic sources of information we may have about likely threats to dams?'

'Um, yes, good point,' pondered the Prime Minister while shouting through to Nathan to come up with an answer. 'Go on.'

'Sir,' started Sir James, trying hard to strike the right balance between instilling confidence and injecting some reality. 'To mount an operation like this would clearly be highly sensitive, but that's a judgement for you. From a military perspective, the best realistic approach to this would in my judgement, Prime Minister…'

'I take it you're not keen?' interjected the Prime Minister incisively.

'It's not my role to question such matters, Sir, merely to advise on their feasibility, resources and likely implications.'

'Indeed, but please continue.'

'I could identify a small number of suitably trained specialist soldiers from ethnically East Asian origin who would blend into a Chinese setting and recce the area and report back. They would need to be armed but in civvies and all speak a variety of Chinese dialects. The principal difficulty here is the sheer size of the country, the number of dams to visit, and the random prospect of being in the right place at the right time.'

'Um, so your conclusion and recommendation?'

'In my judgement, Sir, this is a highly risky proposal with very limited chances of success.'

'OK, Sir James, thank you. I'll need to consult with the Foreign Secretary and consider your comments carefully,' replied the Prime Minister as Nathan emerged hot foot with an answer to the previous question. 'Yes, Nathan?'

'Prime Minister, we do have a limited number of officials in China who do provide some limited intelligence.'

'Say what you mean, Nathan. Do you mean spies?'

'Oh, a very harsh description, Sir. I mean people we can trust in certain positions that would keep us suitably informed if necessary, Sir.'

'Yes, I see. Spies. Thank you, Nathan.'

Chapter Seventeen

Crichton came off the phone after a long conversation with Conrad. He felt quite despondent. How had he arrived at this point, he thought? It had been such a promising start back in Oxford, with such high ideals and such positive intentions, but now he felt like some dubious wheeler dealer in some seedy affair. Much of what he did felt nebulous, chasing shadows, never really knowing the outcome, living on adrenalin, only meeting like-minded people, so narrow and so focussed. He suddenly longed for something else, something more tangible, and something more clear. He felt empty as he reached for a second glass of scotch. *Where will it all end?* he wondered? His thoughts haunted him throughout the day and it was a particularly bad night with crazy dreams and frequent periods of wakefulness, which left him feeling worse as he dragged himself to work that morning. Ruth was obviously concerned and was worried about him.

The journey to work was no relief either, and by the time Crichton had reached the office he felt exhausted. He sat at his desk and went through the motions but the coffee didn't taste as good, the office was too noisy, and the toilets were too shabby. Little things but he felt irritated and uneasy. He couldn't concentrate. He found unnecessary things to do and ignored more urgent matters. This was not good, he knew it was no good, he simply felt that he had to get away, to stop, to think, to consolidate. On the pretext of feeling unwell he left the office early, bought a train ticket to Oxford using his personal not his official card, and started to think about what he would do next.

Crichton was worried that his actions had become immoral, pointless, aimless, and unjustified... a betrayal of his youth. For the first time in his life he almost felt liberated, himself, free thinking, unchained. He walked through the shopping arcade, bought a full set of new clothes, had his hair cut and changed into his new garb leaving his old attire and his *old self*, behind in a safe deposit box on Euston Station. He bought a cheap pay as you go phone, drew out some cash (but not too much to raise suspicion), and boarded the train to Oxford. Crichton felt a sense of boyish excitement as he gazed through the window at the passing landscape, followed by a sense of fear about what he had just done and what the consequences might be.

He arrived in Oxford and booked into a small hotel he remembered in Summertown for two nights. He found an internet café and emailed home from a private email address, leaving a message that he had been called away to a conference at short notice. He said that he would be away a few days and sent a message to work that he was unwell and on medical advice, would need several days off.

For a few hours Crichton Broadhampton-Scott, public school boy, Oxford graduate, senior civil servant, just sat in his room and looked at the wall in silence. Later, he took a bus into town, went first to the KA, then to the Turf and finally to The Crown, where he enjoyed a fine rare fillet steak accompanied by a bottle of good French red wine and felt great. He slept well, rose early for breakfast and set out to walk along the river.

His mind started to clear and Crichton started to address the problem. *I feel out of control,* he told himself. *I feel more than uneasy, I feel positively disgusted at times with the shady compromises, the lies and the mind games.* He thought of love, he thought of his children and his dear wife Ruth. He wanted his mother and he cursed his father. He asked himself what was missing in his life, and the answer was obvious: *meaning.* He continued to indulge with a few pints in The Crown, a casual encounter in a known gay meeting place that helped Crichton feel more in control, more contented. He had always felt quite comfortable with Ruth, although not really attracted, but they were married after all.

By the time he was boarding the train back to reality, Crichton was feeling determined, renewed and resolved. He was confident that his sojourn had been undiscovered and he had decided on a strategy. He reasoned that this was a phase in his life that he had to see it through, but once done, he could consider a change of direction. *Why not?* He had a choice. He could do something completely different. He could consider retirement, move abroad... the possibilities were exciting. *Take control, don't be done to.* The possibilities enhanced his sense of liberation.

As the train moved out of the station, Jan was watching, keeping tabs, took note and left to report to his criminal master for a tidy fee.

Chapter Eighteen

Ahmed by contrast felt confident about what he was doing, or so he thought. He was promoting Arab interests in the world, a task that he felt that he was born to do. It was his place, it was his destiny, it was his right. But there were doubts, there were always doubts. What if ISIS, covertly supported by Saudi Arabia really did follow through with their crazy plan to poison half the West's food and water supplies? Where would that take them? What purpose would it serve?

Crichton arrived back at Euston Station, changed back into his usual office attire, retrieved his normal phone and left his *temporary self* in the safe deposit box, just in case. As he travelled home he practised answering Ruth's inevitable questions about where he had been and the content and conclusions of the conference he hadn't attended.

She didn't disappoint him and he had to deliver his full façade to satisfy her curiosity. The children were pleased to see him and he sat in his usual chair and played the part of the ragged and tired senior civil servant returning from the heavy responsibilities of affairs of state.

Jan reported back to Tak who considered how best to respond to this recent and interesting development – 'a clandestine escape, hey' – he considered. *How can I use this to my advantage?* he thought. *Blackmail perhaps?* He already knew Crichton was gay but didn't consider that there was much mileage in that. *No*, he concluded, there were bigger fish to fry.

'Jan, are the results from following his father still promising?' asked Tak.

'Yes, Tak, they are.'

'You have evidence, photographs?'

'Yes of course,' said Jan.

'Right, so a leak I think. Would the British popular press be interested in a story about a very senior civil servant in a sensitive post, with the immediate ear of the Prime Minister and a champion of the Christian far right who regularly visits known gay pubs and meeting places in Oxford? You bet they would!'

By the following day the story had broken and both Whitehall and Westminster were in crisis. This was not good timing. Furious and strenuous denials and cries of complaint about the irresponsibility of the press followed, countered by stoic defence of the right of freedom of speech. The government, the party, the Christian right, the gay community, Oxford to name but a few were all seriously offended, not to mention Toby Broadhampton-Scott himself. Inevitable questions were raised about the judgement of the senior official and demands for the Prime Minister to act immediately by ordering his replacement. The police had to be involved, although even before they started their enquiries, very strong messages were being sent to deter them that this was a matter of national security and not in the public interest.

Whilst the events played out, Crichton observed in horror. How could this be that his holier than thou father, Bastian of morality, could possibly have managed to get himself embroiled in such a situation? This had been compounded of course by Crichton's own uncomfortable history of never feeling able to even broach the subject of his own sexuality with his father. An issue that had effectively destroyed what little hope they had ever had of having a reasonable family relationship.

This was exactly what Tak had intended and in so doing only added to Crichton's current malaise and reduced his efficiency still further, thereby weakening the official machinery aimed at countering the threat from ISIS. As a result he was paid handsomely for his endeavours and for the risks involved before he and Jan quickly left the country by pre-arranged private jet.

Chapter Nineteen

London

Not only team members but more senior staff had begun to notice Crichton's sudden crisis of conscience and dip in efficiency. This was not the time. It would never be the time. There was never a good time for such behaviour. Loyalty was expected; weakness was not. This wasn't about Crichton's own sexuality, which was common knowledge and regarded as his private business. It was also known that he wasn't generally active and, at least on the surface, he was a happily married man. And that's all that mattered. No, the main concern was that he clearly was not on board, was not performing at a crucial time, and that could not continue.

The intelligence community were buzzing. Information was coming in fast and Crichton, with all his misgivings, was at the heart of it. Staff were racing around, phones were active and all forms of secure communication were being fully engaged. Liaison across government departments had been streamlined for this operation and regular communication was being maintained with other leading European states and with America.

'Are we ready? Because every indication we have is that they are coming,' asked a senior official accompanied by a cabinet minister.

'Yes, intelligence certainly suggests an increase in threat level. Matters are now critical. We believe that ISIS has grown tired of the West's procrastinations and are getting restless for action. It can't be long now before they strike, or attempt to.'

'What further actions have we taken to counter the threat?' asked the Minister.

'Sir, state security services across the West are braced to pounce at the slightest opportunity in order to prevent any threat to our food or water integrity. There have been several attempts already that have been intercepted,' responded Crichton.

'Well, that's good but realistically they will get through somewhere at some point, won't they?' posed the Minister.

'Yes, that is always the fear,' replied an MI5 officer.

'Um, we need to do more to prepare the public for this inevitability. Do you guys need anything else at this point?' he concluded.

'We will ask if we do, Sir.'

'OK, I'll go and brief the Prime Minister. He will probably want to call his own meeting.' At this point he left whilst the frenzied activity continued.

The intelligence boys continued to talk amongst themselves.

'Have we really got enough resources on our side to defeat them, that's the question?' continued one official.

'When it comes to it will other European nations act or vacillate?' asked another.

'It's difficult to tell, to be sure. We are in uncharted territory here! At the end of the day, we are here to protect British interests and although all other countries would deny it in public as we would, their own national interests will come first too. We'll cooperate if we can, but don't worry if we can't, I don't,' concluded the team leader.

New York

'More messages from the Brits, George. They anticipate another meeting and want to consult us first.'

'OK, what about?'

'Coordinating strategy, I suppose?'

'We're getting past the stage of grand plans now, Brad. We really must prepare to act. What are we missing? That's what bothers me. Where are the gaps?'

'We know their broad intentions and we sense it's imminent. We know they have sleepers across Europe – some that we know about and some that we don't – and we know they have the expertise, including Hilary Jameson…'

'That's it,' said George, 'we know all that, but we don't

know the precise details; the where, the when, and the who? That's what we don't know! Where are they storing this stuff? We still haven't discovered their source or traced their supply chain in any detail. Nor do we know for certain if Europe really is the prime target and what is the direct level of threat to the US?

'I also wonder how close the link is between green activists and ISIS. An unlikely alliance don't you think? Do the Brits know if they really are cooperating, or who is using who, or have we just got this aspect completely wrong? Have ISIS somehow become aware of the threats made by the Green Alliance and seized upon a weakness in Western defences? We'll probably never know. It's messy, but it's always messy.'

Cobra, London

'Thank you all for your attendance at such short notice. I just felt it was the right time to bring us back together,' opened the Prime Minister. 'It seems there have been developments and therefore we have to be prepared for a serious threat.

'So, if I can summarise. I have consulted with other Western heads of government this morning, and all the indications are of an imminent attack. Plans are in hand to various degrees to combat that threat and we are pretty confident that we can.' There were nods, mostly more out of etiquette than genuine confidence.

The Prime Minister continued: 'Our friends in the USA advise me that their intelligence picture is still missing the details; the precise where, the when, and the who? We also agreed that we need to up our efforts to warn and prepare the public, both out of political expediency and to avoid mass panic. The question then is how can we secure any of that detail... any ideas?'

Discussion ensued and options were generated, concluding with tasking several key people to develop those ideas into something more concrete.

Before the meeting ended one of the members asked: 'Prime Minister, is Europe the priority now? Are we less concerned about the potential threat to the USA or China at this point?'

'Yes, realistically we are,' was the reply.

***

Crichton knew that they had to respond to the instructions from Cobra but at the moment couldn't help feeling distracted more by the issues surrounding his father. They had only exchanged words briefly and on one occasion since the explosive story had broken. Crichton sensed that he at least owed that much to his father, to support and to defend him now when he needed it most, and decided it was time to meet.

He was both pleased and slightly surprised by his father's prompt reply and invitation to coffee that morning in his private office. Crichton felt compelled to attend. As he walked across London it felt like being summoned as he had as a schoolboy, to meet his father at the end of term when travelling between school and home. While the issues were different this time round, he still felt very much the junior partner when facing his formidable father. Knowing that his father couldn't be gay, he wondered if his father had ever considered that he was; after all, they had never had the conversation. He thought how he could strike the right tone, how he could reinforce his father's sense of injustice and offer to help restore his reputation. Yes, that was what needed to be done.

As he entered the government building, satisfied security and climbed the stairs to the second floor, Crichton certainly felt some sense of anticipation. Before he knocked on the heavy oak door, his father opened it and beckoned him inside the large and formal room. After pleasantries and coffee, the conversation somewhat awkwardly turned to the principal issue at stake.

'Father, I feel so desperately sorry that you have had to

endure such awful public accusation. Completely without foundation, it must have been so difficult for you. I'm sure you can compose a statesman-like repost and start to rebuild your position and reputation.'

'No, Crichton. I can't do that, I'm afraid.'

'Oh and why ever not?' Crichton replied bemused.

'Because it's true.'

Crichton felt like the foundations of his whole world had just shifted. Surely not. How could this be? he thought. He was not concerned by moral indignation but by the sheer hypocrisy of his father's frequent and often very public pronouncements, decrying and denying the very existence of varied sexual orientations. How that had compounded his own very real agonies about his own feelings, horror, shame and disgust as he grew up before eventually coming to terms with who he was and finding friends who readily accepted it without issue.

As his father stood rigid in the middle of the office where his admission had been issued, Crichton felt that he must leave, and turning his back, wondered if he could ever address his father again. He took the lift and in his shock proceeded to the top floor before finding the correct buttons to bring him back to ground to facilitate his departure from the building.

Walking back across London was a blur. As he returned to his own office, affairs of state had to take immediate priority. In a private meeting his immediate superior – not knowing of course of the interaction Crichton had just had – felt that he could not avoid the issue any longer.

He looked up and spoke: 'Crichton, I feel I must speak with you. We have tried to be understanding and we have been patient… but now I really must insist that you shake off whatever it is that's preoccupying your mind, and come back on board for the sake of national interest.'

Still somewhat shaken, Crichton stumbled into a reply: 'Yes, Sir. I agree. I understand… yes, I'm with you.'

'In a nutshell, what has been the problem?'

'Well, situations and people are not always what they

seem and at times that can be disconcerting,' Crichton uttered with stoic understatement.

'Yes indeed, I see. Now can we get on, you need to make contact with Conrad again and get some details of the likely impact of poisoning using the substances we are aware of, to various concentrations. That's your immediate priority.'

Crichton nodded knowing that the brief consultation was over. In a perverse way his father's interjection had helped him to refocus on what was important. Crichton committed to himself to put his demons to one side for now and concentrate on the immediate threat to Western civilisation. After all, what was he agonising about compared to that?

In a passing conversation the Prime Minister was assured that Crichton Broadhampton-Scott was now fully restored and would report back his findings from Professor Lindstrand in due course.

***

With new determination Crichton contacted Conrad.

'Hi, Conrad, how are things?'

'Good and you?'

'Yes, I've been tasked to update our knowledge on the potential impact of the poisoning threat.'

'Yes, I have done some work on this to advise the UN and reviewed available data. I have summarised this in a briefing paper, which has just gone out today via secure means. In essence, the conclusion is that as regards water, we know what chemical they have and there is a neutralising agent and stocks have been distributed.'

'So, that's not too bad?' asked Crichton.

'No, relatively speaking,' said Conrad. 'The problem is that you can't use the neutralising agent as a precautionary measure and we won't know where and when the poison has been applied until symptoms are reported and then it's too late, at least for those already affected.'

'I see, and what are the likely symptoms?'

'Anything from mild stomach upset through chronic

sickness and diarrhoea to death I'm afraid... depending on the concentration used.'

'And the potential impact on the food chain?'

'Now, this is far more difficult,' said Conrad. 'There are many potential means to infiltrate the food chain; some with devastating immediate effect, and others with more likely longer-term impact. I'm afraid they are more difficult to predict, detect or prevent. Some examples and details are in my paper, but I warn you it makes chilling reading.'

After, any more personal conversation seemed inappropriate and both men returned to their respective duties promptly. Crichton was definitely feeling more focused but his demons still haunted him, and all he could do was to try to put them aside for the time being.

Chapter Twenty

London

Pressure was mounting. The intelligence community were highly vocal pressing for action, and delay was inevitably political. High level talks continued. Matters were delicate. Whilst the public needed to be forewarned to some extent, too much would create unnecessary anxiety and effectively handing over a PR victory to the terrorists. Too little, risked being caught unprepared. The balance was tricky, but time was running out.

Both the Green Alliance and ISIS had made ultimatums and set deadlines. Quite how far these were coordinated, separate or just unconnected, was still not clear. But if they meant what they said there was now little more than two days before potential disaster across Europe and possibly beyond. Analysis, judgment and the best hunches available doubted that ultimately a coalition of green interests could actually coordinate attacks on this scale. It was felt more likely that ISIS was the principal threat and choice of an environmental means of attack was more born of opportunism than any commitment to green politics.

In a small private dark room, a few of the most senior people sat having reviewed Conrad's paper. The mood was serious and the atmosphere tense. After a while the emphasis shifted to how to achieve an edge. How to secure an advantage at this stage? It was agreed that the edge they needed was information. How to acquire it was the question. What were their options? A consensus readily emerged that in these circumstances information had to come from the inside. Available intelligence from existing agents was limited, but there was one source that they could employ with reasonable prospects of some progress. Yes, they were agreed, it was time to use Crichton's link with Ahmed. It was time to discover whether the years of nurturing this relationship and contact would finally pay dividends. They knew, however, that once used it would be compromised, so there was only one chance to make it work and they decided it was time to take it.

The detail was delegated to the intelligence and operations group, who quickly worked on a plan of action. It was a high risk strategy, but somehow they needed to demonstrate to Ahmed just how serious this matter had become, on the assumption that he was not fully aware. Then, they would appeal to his sense of morality and what loyalty he had left to Crichton and his time spent studying in the West, and seek his assistance to help avert potential disaster.

A message to that effect was drawn up, revised checked and checked again.

Riyadh, Saudi Arabia

In his position in Saudi Arabia, Ahmed was feeling uncomfortable. He was not party to the highest echelon of government where the real decisions were made and was not sure exactly what the shady relationship was between his government and ISIS, other than he suspected that it involved tacit support and some funding.

He was concerned about the threat posed by ISIS expanding into China and feared that it could unleash severe unintended consequences. The Chinese would inevitably be tested at some point in their emerging position in the new world order, but he considered that this was neither the time nor the place. The central question he was posing to himself was whether this action into China was likely to result in benefit or loss to Arab interests in the world? Frankly, he wasn't sure and that was not the position he wanted to be in. It could go either way and therefore was inherently risky. *Too risky?* he asked himself.

The internal wrestle with conscience, how it plagued him, how it wrangled. Loyalty to who, to what versus a greater moral dimension, was that the question? The consequences of action versus the consequences of inaction, nothing seemed straight forward, nothing seemed really clear.

Ahmed was also acutely aware that his position was precarious. The state forces who monitored him would not hesitate to act on a whim. He often thought how he might handle it if he had to and what to do about his family – what to do for the best? He had made some preliminary enquires about safe custody if circumstances dictated the need, but he knew that no hiding place would ever be secure. He put such thoughts to the back of his mind, trying to convince himself that he would never need such provision.

London

With now less than forty-eight hours until the first deadline, there was a sense of urgency in the camp. The draft message to Ahmed was ready. Basically, it described the scenario and sought his opinion on how real it was. It was written as a private note between friends, no more, and an awful lot hung on its outcome.

Crichton was called to his superior's office. He knew in the context of the day that this summons would have to be of key importance. He speculated on what exactly was that important as he climbed the stairs as quickly as he could to respond. As he entered the office, Crichton could sense the atmosphere, the tension, the anticipation.

'Sit down, Crichton. We have decided it is time to make a brave and critical call that only you can execute.'

Crichton was puzzled, flattered in a way but expected a fall to follow. What would this be, he wondered, and why only him?

'Crichton, you know that your lasting communication with Ahmed Salib has been important to us in a number of ways. Now, that time is running out; we need to take a risk and ask him directly for help, and that's why it has to come from you.'

'What sort of help?' responded Crichton anxiously.

'To ask him directly if the threat is credible.'

Silence fell in the room as Crichton tried to absorb the significance of what he'd just heard. 'As open as that?' he enquired.

'Yes, because he is our only contact who is likely to know. None of our other sources give us a clear enough picture to justify immediate action. We need to know how far this threat comes from ISIS. Or, is this a front for wider Middle Eastern ambitions, from the Arab world against the West, the Chinese, or both.'

'But what makes you so confident that he will be party to this, or prepared to share it with us?'

'Simply because it's the best and increasingly the only chance we have left.'

'But you realise the dangers involved,' said Crichton, 'and the likely consequences?'

'Yes we do, but this is imminent now, Crichton, and it's time to use your contact to ask the vital question after all these years of developing trust.'

'Even though it will certainly cost him his life?'

'Yes.'

'And those of his family?'

'I'm afraid so.'

Crichton felt upset, angry and confused. This was not what he had expected. He was ordered to send the message now, placing him in the most extreme dilemma of his life. To obey the demands of his role, his career, to serve the supposed interests of his country, but to betray a friend and his family, leaving them in imminent danger, which would inevitably result in their death. How much would Ahmed really know, he thought, and could he actually answer the question? And, even if he did, could they trust his reply? The answer to neither question seemed at all certain. A passing thought returned to him of a previous conversation; in fact, the last face-to-face conversation he had with Ahmed, when he made the strange statement that they could stop this madness. *Is that what he meant?* he wondered. *Is that what he was alluding too?* He didn't know. He felt confused. Nothing seemed certain, yet everything seemed questionable.

Thoughts raced through his mind as he sat in front of his secure computer. All the recent troubles, all the angst had returned, all the uncertainties all the moral dilemmas. Crichton froze, but he knew the answer instinctively.

'Send it now,' came the instruction.

'I can't. I can't do it,' he replied.

'You must, it has to be you. You have the codes. You are the one who is authorised. You are the only one he'll trust.'

'I can't. I really can't…'

'For God's sake man, do it!' shouted his superior, starting to lose control.

Whilst Crichton hesitated, his fuming superior left the room through a side door to meet Ruth.

'Damn it! You'll have to go in there and convince him yourself, Ruth.'

'But that will…'

'Yes, I know, but we simply can't wait any longer.'

Ruth slowly entered the office, pushing back the door carefully.

'Ruth. Not now darling.'

'Crichton, I know the situation, you must send the message.'

'But, Ahmed will die if I do.'

'Yes, and potentially thousands will die if you don't,' she said.

'So they tell me,' said Crichton. 'Do you believe them?'

'Yes.'

'Then I really have no choice.'

'No.'

There was a pause for reflection before Crichton asked: 'So, did you ever work in the city?'

'No,' she said. 'Not really.'

'And all those meetings and trips away weren't actually charitable works then?'

'No.'

'I guess your real name isn't really Patel either, Ruth?'

'Actually, it is. I kept it regardless, but I wasn't adopted by an English family. My parents were early victims of ISIS, as they rampaged through Afghanistan, Pakistan and India when the conflict started.'

'They were killed and that's when you were recruited?'

'Yes, just two months before starting at Oxford.'

'And you've been my handler ever since?'

'No, Crichton, it wasn't like that. It wasn't until much later that that became necessary. My feelings for you have always been genuine and as I have described to you.'

'Ruth, I feel I've been manipulated all my life.'

'Yes, dear, that's right.'

After a long silence, she continued: 'But this is different, Crichton. This is stark reality and it's your chance to be genuine, to be yourself. Think what's important here and the actions you must take will be obvious to you. Do it because it needs to be done, not because you see it as manipulation. Crichton, do it because in the circumstances it's the only option left. Do it because it's right, and then you will be able to live with it afterwards.'

Crichton looked up at her knowing that she was right, accepting that she usually was. Ultimately, this was not about dominance, or world order, or even East versus West. As far as he was concerned, it was about humanity and that thousands or even millions of people could die from a series of catastrophic events. If nothing else, surely it wasn't about himself and Ahmed.

'OK, Ruth, leave me now. I'll write and send it.'

She gestured to object but he interjected.

'No,' he replied assertively. 'I have to write this myself.'

Accepting what he said on this occasion, Ruth left him to his work. Her job done, her position had now expired, but she remained in hope that her marriage would survive.

Reluctantly, with a heavy heart, Crichton sat down with the official draft to compose an emotional and very personal note to a dying friend. He referred to their Oxford days, their lofty ambitions, their aspirations, and their great moral and philosophical debates. He appealed to the heart, asking

Ahmed to do as he was doing, and to do the right thing, regardless of the personal cost.

Taking the precaution of a last minute code change, Crichton sent the message with its secret encryption.

Chapter Twenty-One

Riyadh, Saudi Arabia

Thirty-six hours to the deadline

Sitting alone in his office late at night, Ahmed received the message from Crichton. As he read it, he knew for sure that it could have come from no other source. He read the words and felt the emotion in his message. He acknowledged the essence of what Crichton was saying. He read it again and again with tears in his eyes, and he knew that it was right.

So, was the threat credible, he asked himself? And was it as imminent as they feared? He checked again: thirty-six hours! No, he couldn't believe it. He wasn't aware or had been made aware of this to this extent, but he knew he had to find out more, in order to try to uncover the truth. Despite their different perspectives and the different directions their lives had taken, this wasn't fundamentally about politics, Western or Middle Eastern interests, history or mistrust… this was far deeper. In the intensity of that moment and despite the wider implications, this was about helping a friend.

Ahmed left his office in the early hours of the morning after instigating his plans to secure the safety of his family, and attempting to grab a few hours' fitful sleep. What had been happening here? Who was behind this evil alliance with ISIS? How high did the corruption go? He had no answers. Whilst he pondered, one of his mobile phones buzzed in his pocket. One not often used. His presence was required, *why so early?* Ahmed was being summoned to a meeting, not unusual in itself, but this meeting was. The message indicated a meeting of the select few, the chosen ones, the ones who would rule after the West was cowed. Early hours, secret location, favoured few, the signs were ominous. *Why him?* Had they invited the wrong person? Had he picked up the wrong phone in his haste and panic to leave the office? He wasn't sure. Nothing seemed to make sense anymore.

Now he knew that Crichton's concerns were justified. Had he missed the warning signs? Had there been any? Whatever the answer to these questions, Ahmed knew that his destiny lay in attending or infiltrating this meeting. Would he be expected? What would be the security arrangements? Questions, thoughts, anxieties all flowed through his mind as he approached the venue.

Despite his anxieties, fervour and excitement seemed to dominate the air. Wearing a traditional Arab dress, he entered a discreet meeting room in a place that he recognised would not attract undue attention.

As Ahmed looked around the room, he saw some familiar faces, but also a few surprises. He avoided eye contact. It felt like he had been invited to a celebration before the event had taken place. That was if the actions Crichton had described were to be implemented. The room was private and secure and the presentation both vitriolic and dramatic. In the short address, generations of resentment of Western interference, imperialism and domination were evident with an intensity and with a passion that were as infectious as they were alarming. Ahmed was stunned. The implications of this were far wider than he had imagined. He was horrified. He realised that he was sitting in a room with those who perceived that they would emerge after ISIS had done their dirty work. That the West would be provoked into an extension of the murky and unsatisfactory 'war on terror' and would be so weakened having eliminated the unworthy allies of those present in this room, to leave them free to take centre stage in a new world order. How improbable, how naive, how dangerous.

As the presentation concluded with cheers and chants, those wishing to enhance their bids for influence flocked to the top table as Ahmed noticed a file that was lying on the edge of the front table. Could he? He wondered if it would be possible. Unnoticed in the frenzy, he moved forward and quickly covered the file and secured it under his thawb, the long Arab gown. Moving swiftly away, Ahmed new this was his chance. There was a greater loyalty, a loyalty to humanity itself. ISIS was not the answer, it was evil and it had to be stopped, and any shady radical group fronting it. As he thought of the implications, he became more determined. He was conscious of the time constraints and felt it was right to take another risk.

Normal means were too risky now, so he drove a pool diplomatic car to the British embassy. Clutching the file, he ran into the building only to find boxes, frantic packing and a sense of disintegration.

'Where's the ambassador?' he demanded. 'I must speak with him now.'

'You'll be lucky,' replied the lowly official. 'I'm not sure if he's still here, mate. Most of the staff were flown out yesterday.'

'But I must see him urgently,' cried Ahmed. 'It's vital!'

A man emerged from the interior of the building to introduce himself. 'I'm Sir Andrew Windsor-Hague, the British ambassador. What can I do for you?'

Ahmed recognised him as one of Ruth's cousins, a few years older than them, but a Cambridge man he thought. Ahmed quickly explained the significance of the secret file and the sense of urgency, which the ambassador could recognise immediately. Without delay he was able to send it by diplomatic secure means to London for Crichton's immediate attention.

Ahmed felt such a sense of relief, then fear. Would he be apprehended before he could complete what he knew he must do next?

London

Less than twenty-four hours to the deadline

Crichton received the document and immediately realised its significance. He rushed to the heart of government knowing that this required immediate action.

The file contained details of the terrorist plot; names, locations, means, sources of supply and distribution... all the details of a plan to strike a critical blow at Europe's food and water supplies. America was identified as a secondary target. Fortunately, there was no further mention of the use of dirty bombs to inhibit any civil authorities in their attempts to intervene, although of course, that didn't guarantee anything. Neither was there any further mention of China.

The Prime Minister viewed the evidence in front of him and immediately shouted to Nathan his faithful private secretary, to call for the Head of the Armed Services to help him decide his next move. As expected, he arrived almost instantly.

'Prime Minister, you require my assistance?'

'Yes, Sir James. Nathan has told you about the file?'

'Yes, and the sense of urgency. Your question, Prime Minister?'

'The factory manufacturing the poison chemical is based nowhere near where we expected. We thought it had to be in the Middle East, but in fact it's in Central Africa. I'm concerned about the potential threat from dirty bombs. Remember the New York incident?' Sir James nodded. 'At the time we believed that it was probably a dry run, to prove the method for a bigger hit later. I'm concerned: is this the bigger hit? Are we to face dirty bombs potentially at every incident site to disrupt our relief efforts?'

'Other than the New York incident, is there any hard evidence to support that concern?' asked Sir James.

'No. I don't believe so.'

'Nothing in the file, that's otherwise so comprehensive?'

'No.'

'Then we can't chase shadows, Prime Minister. I'd advise that we act on what we know.'

'But we might be wrong and that would be catastrophic!'

'Intelligence is never fact, Prime Minister, but it's the best information we have and we have to be decisive... we can't delay.'

'No indeed, I just wondered how close are your nearest special forces who could check out the factory for us?'

'No, Prime Minister, there simply isn't time. My nearest troops are deployed across North Africa. But to arrange a move, brief them, plan, access the area through hostile and unstable country in difficult terrain, would just take too long and wouldn't guarantee a satisfactory answer anyway. We know where the chemical factory is now but a dirty bomb could be made anywhere in the world, and probably not there.'

'Yes, I see. So your professional advice is to go ahead and take the risk?'

'From a military perspective, yes, Prime Minister. However, the political judgement is yours.'

The Prime Minister handed him the file with instructions to act. There were sensitivities here about parliamentary consultation, but the Prime Minister considered that he had to act decisively. Because of the circumstances, he could defend that approach and deal with any repercussions later, gambling that if he was successful, that there wouldn't be any such complications. A risk, he acknowledged to himself, but one that he felt confident was the right course of action.

Within hours missiles were in the air to designated targets, dawn arrests across Europe were taking place and security was being beefed up at all key sites. It was a massive operation, but one that had been prepared to some degree, ready to implement with the right information.

Riyadh, Saudi Arabia

Ahmed moved through the streets on foot, carefully looking around him, always fearing the worst. He was about to take the biggest gamble of his life, but one that he felt was likely to be justified. He carried on through the streets as the city became alive, more people to mingle with, less chance of identification or being apprehended, he kept telling himself.

He noticed a man behind him: *was he following him?* He wasn't sure. He quickened his pace, took a few sharp turns, doubled back and appeared to have lost his shadow. *Not far now*, he thought as the streets seemed to get longer, and there in the distance was his target.

On arrival at the entrance to the royal palace, Ahmed knew that he had to convince the security staff of his legitimacy, knowing that if he had calculated wrongly and they were already looking for him, then he would simply have played into their hands. He passed through the first check point without a problem using basic ID. At the second check point, he needed to apply some persuasion, and succeeded, but by the third check point his luck had ran out. The guard surveyed him critically, listened to his request but remained sceptical. He went away to seek higher authority, and then returned a short while later.

'You say you *demand* to see the King?'

'Yes, that's right,' said Ahmed. 'It's most important and most urgent.'

'My friend, you do not demand to see a King. He summons you, if required. You must state your business.'

'It is for the King's ears only.'

'Then you must turn around and leave,' insisted the stern guard. A more senior guard arrived and the argument continued. Ahmed was getting frustrated, knowing that the clock was ticking and vital time was ebbing away. He wondered how he could convince them without appearing to be desperate and attract the wrong attention.

Then, through the courtyard in front of him, an entourage came into view, which proceeded in his direction with some urgency. Ahmed felt sure that the King was at the rear of the group. Now was his chance. Now was his moment. He had to make a move before the guards deemed him to be too much of a risk; perhaps they had already assumed he was a suicide bomber, in which case, he knew that they could shoot him at any moment without question.

As the group got nearer he was able to recognise one of the King's party and caught his eye.

'Ahmed, what are you doing here at this time?' he enquired.

'Wasim, I must speak with the King. It's vital!' he cried.

Wasim knew of Ahmed's position and that whilst unusual, he felt that his request was unlikely to be unwarranted. The King became aware of the exchange and sought confirmation from another of his officials. Wasim explained to the King Ahmed's position and that his request maybe significant. From the mood of the party, Ahmed judged that something had already happened to alert them.

The King seemed concerned that one of his senior subjects was so troubled at this time and beckoned to the guards to let him through. The King and his senior officials listened with interest as Ahmed started to convey his concerns and felt reassured that it seemed evident, as he had hoped, that the King had not been made fully aware of the apparent links with ISIS, let alone been complicit. What Ahmed had to tell him simply confirmed his early suspicions about certain elements within his own government, although this was evidently far more serious than he had at first envisaged.

As the news broke to the world of a timely international intervention to intercept the misguided actions of a combination of extreme radical elements, the King acted decisively to attempt to put his house in order. Arrests were swift and retribution brutal and unforgiving.

Postscript

There was no Green Terror attack on either America or China. Whilst across Europe some actions did get through they were minor and their impact on local people minimal. Much to the authorities' relief, there were no incidents recorded involving the use of dirty bombs. Key protagonists were arrested and food and water sites secured.

Due to the threat of delayed impact, the authorities remained jittery for a while, however, there were no immediate risks. Nonetheless the prospect of longer-term damage by actions taken and yet undetected still remained.

For the Oxford friends, the impact of the incident and all its implications lived on. Crichton decided the time was right to move on and risk a change of direction and a new career. He went into journalism covering foreign affairs. He considered how best to respond to Ruth, given her recent revelation. On balance, Crichton felt that he still loved her and that he had no other relationships or unfulfilled intentions in the background yearning to emerge. He found comfort in her support and thought that she had only done what she felt was right at the time.

Ruth was initially surprised when Crichton approached her to discuss his feelings and that he didn't want to separate, but wanted to stay together and felt that they could work it out. She was pleased nevertheless and had similar thoughts. Their relationship had always been pragmatic; a compromise, but there was nothing wrong with that. She wondered whether it was now too late to return to her ambition to work in finance in the city and concluded that it probably was, so she decided to take some time off to consider what to do next. There were options and there was no hurry. The children were secure in good schools and between them they had always been high earners, and they had reserves, so there was no pressure or rush to make financial adjustments.

Crichton was relieved that his worst fears of the potential impact on his friend Ahmed had not materialised. His feelings, however, were more than mere relief. He felt renewed and reinvigorated by the results of his actions, and his conscience had a change of direction. At last he felt free to follow his heart.

Conrad and Hayley continued to be deeply in love and did take the time to have a family in between international travel and commitments. They continued to be active in green politics and to promote the cause of sustainability.

Ahmed was expected to remain stoic in his senior position in the Saudi establishment. His family had remained safe during the recent events and they were able to return to their comfortable family home. He accepted his role and responsibilities and felt that his job was not yet complete in trying to influence East–West relations for the good and play a part in establishing an emerging new world order.

Unsurprisingly, Arabella had achieved her life's ambitions and was an establishment celebrity married to a high profile artist and was free to grace many an elaborate and irrelevant society event. She had experienced many loves including Ahmed whom she just managed to remember from time to time.

International insecurity of course continued with the existence of significant threats both old and new. Some of those who chose to operate outside the law were detained and incarcerated, but others remained free, including Hilary Jameson.